The Co the Cabana

Viola Roberts Cozy Mysteries:
Book 1

Shéa MacLeod

The Corpse in the Cabana
Viola Roberts Cozy Mysteries: Book 1
Text copyright © 2016 Shéa MacLeod
All rights reserved.
Printed in the United States of America.

Cover Art by Amanda Kelsey of Razzle Dazzle Designs
Editing by Janet Fix of www.thewordverve.com
Proofing by Jenx Byron
Formatted by PyperPress

Dedication

This one's for my mom. I promised I'd write a book you could read. One without scary vampires and whatnot. Well, here it is.

Shéa MacLeod

Acknowledgments

With a HUGE thanks to Cheryl Bradshaw and Diane Capri who insisted over cocktails that I really should write that cozy mystery I'd always wanted to write.

Also thanks to the Big Girl Panties who have cheered me on through the whole process.

Thanks to my inspiration, Agatha Christie, for penning such wonderful tales of mayhem and murder. If you're out there somewhere, you changed my life.

To my marvelous critique partners, editors, and proofreaders who make every book shine.

And to A for putting up with my crazy. I love you.

Shéa MacLeod

Chapter 1
The Second Most Haunted Building in Florida

"If you look over there on your left, you'll see the Don CeSar Hotel. It's the second most haunted building in all of Florida," the taxi driver declared proudly, as if he, personally, was responsible for the ghosts and their shenanigans.

"The pink one?" Cheryl Delaney, my best friend and fellow author, craned her neck to see out the window. We were on our way to the Fairwinds Resort for a writer's conference, and I was feeling more than a little punch drunk from the travel. The flight from Portland, Oregon, took nearly eight hours, and I was still drowsy from the airsickness medicine. "Yep. That's the one," the driver said cheerfully. He adjusted his sunglasses on his ruddy nose and ran a hand through thinning hair.

I peered around Cheryl to see an enormous art deco-style building looming against the harsh, blue sky. Sure enough, it was pink. Pepto-Bismol pink, to be exact. I half wished we were staying there, ghosts or no ghosts. At least the place had character, unlike the rest of the resorts marching their way down the coast of St. Petersburg, Florida. They looked like something out of a bad sixties sci-fi movie, their ugly "futuristic" hulks hovering over the water like spacecraft.

I didn't expect a haunted mansion to be painted Pepto-Bismol pink. Like most people, I expected a haunted place to be gloomy, dark, and atmospheric. The Don CeSar Hotel was not your usual haunted mansion.

"I know all kinds of people who've had run-ins with ghosts there," the taxi driver continued. "They say the ghost of the first owner still walks the grounds."

"Oh, how exciting," Cheryl said with a shiver. "Maybe we'll see him."

I might be a lover of murder mysteries, but I draw the line at ghosts. Cheryl could ghost hunt all she wanted. I was staying away from anything remotely spooky.

# # #

"Get a load of her." Cheryl Delaney nearly dumped her wine all over the polished marble floor as she gestured wildly at one of the women on the dance floor. It was the kickoff party for the Novel Writers of America conference. Being writers, half the NWA Conference attendees were already three sheets to the wind, even though it was barely nine o'clock. "She does know she's old enough to be his mother, right?"

I tracked the dancers as they glided, bobbed, and lurched across the polished wood dance floor. Above them bobbed blue and silver balloons filled with helium while an '80s number thumped over the loudspeakers, loud enough to make my head throb. We'd just flown in from Portland mere hours before, and what I wanted more than anything was a nap. Instead I was stuck at a meet-and-greet.

I finally found the woman Cheryl was pointing to. She was at least in her early fifties, although well preserved and expensively dressed, and was draped drunkenly on a man at least half her age. Wasn't the first time I'd seen such behavior at a writer's conference or from the woman in question. I snorted. Partially in amusement, partially in derision.

"Natasha Winters is a lush." I kept my voice low. Gossip spread like wildfire among writers, especially those of the romance variety. The last thing I needed was Natasha getting angry at me. "Unfortunately, she could also outsell us ten times over."

"Figures," Cheryl sighed, sucking down half her Mai Tai in one gulp. She'd gelled her short, brown hair so it stood up in spikes. Anyone else would have looked like a rabid squirrel. On Cheryl, the look was cute. "Not that I'm complaining. Sales have been good this year, but really…Why do the nasty ones always get the world handed to them on a silver platter?" She glanced around for a waiter, empty wineglass dangling from one hand.

It was a good question. I mean, Natasha Winters was nice enough, all things considered, but she was a major diva, a drunk, and a total cougar. The kind of woman who made everyone cringe. It was sort of embarrassing, actually, the way she carried on. I was of the opinion that a certain decorum was required of professional writers. A decorum Natasha was sadly lacking. She also happened to be the number-one best-selling romance writer. The woman was raking in money hand over fist. I couldn't help a small pang of jealousy, which I ruthlessly squashed. I was of the mind that when it came to writing, there were plenty of readers for everyone, and while it would have been nice to have the kind of seven-figure income writers like Natasha Winters commanded, I was perfectly happy with my very comfortable, although less impressive, income.

"Viola Roberts, how lovely to finally meet you." A deep voice interrupted my train of thought, jerking my attention from Natasha and her gyrating boy toy to the man who'd suddenly appeared next to me.

He was tall, over six feet, and gorgeous in a distinguished older man sort of way. *Not that much older*, I reminded myself. My forty-second birthday was just around the corner and Mr. Gorgeous looked no more than late forties. Possibly very early fifties. He had a slight accent that could have been British…or maybe something else. It was hard to tell. His piercing gray eyes crinkled slightly at the corners, the laugh lines sexy rather than aging. *Be still my heart.*

Beside me, Cheryl went dead still, zeroing in on the newcomer. She looked ready to burst with excitement, practically bouncing in her nude-colored heels. Obviously she knew who the gentleman was, which left me at a distinct disadvantage.

I quirked an eyebrow, giving him the once-over. He was very elegantly dressed in a black suit and matching shirt and tie. "And you are?" It probably came out a little snottier than I meant it. Cheryl nearly choked before gesturing wildly to the waiter.

"Lucas Salvatore." He gave an elegant little bow that on anyone else would have been ridiculous. On him it was...sexy. Very European. "I'm a huge fan of your work."

The waiter moved just close enough for Cheryl to snag another glass of wine off his tray. She clutched it like a lifeline, eyes darting between me and Salvatore like she was watching a tennis match.

My other eyebrow went up. "Oh, really? Which work in particular?" I seriously doubted this Lucas Salvatore person had read anything of mine. He wasn't exactly in my demographic.

His smile widened, pearly whites bright against darkly tanned skin. "*The Cowboy's Lost Mistress* was an enjoyable tale. I read it on the plane."

"Uh huh." I wrote historical romance novels. The kind that involved a great deal of heaving bosoms and ripping bodices and cowboys who were overly fond of tearing their shirts off. I had a hard time picturing Salvatore as being into that sort of thing. And why did his name sound so familiar? I racked my brain but came up empty.

"Honestly," he said, "it was a lot of fun."

"Thank you." What else to say? I'd learned to take compliments about my writing, no matter how bizarre, with as much grace as humanly possible. "And what do you write, Mr. Salvatore?" I asked with mild interest. I guessed he was a writer since he was at a writer's conference.

Cheryl flailed, face going an interesting shade of purple. I could only assume she was familiar with his work, but his name still wasn't ringing any bells.

His smile was genuine with perhaps a trace of self-mockery. Obviously he didn't take himself too seriously. Good. There were plenty of that sort already. Like the aforementioned Natasha Winters. Writers as a whole tended to be rather full of themselves.

"Call me Lucas. I dabble in thrillers mostly," he said, eyeing me over the rim of his glass. He was drinking an Old Fashioned. Whiskey, from the look of it. Not really my cup of tea, so to speak.

"Ah." Color me not surprised. He looked the sort for thrillers. Heck, eighty percent of the men attending NWA wrote thrillers. I'd bet he was an ex-cop or something.

A particularly loud and obnoxious laugh from the dance floor drew our attention back to Natasha Winters. Her top was a bit askew, showing an alarming amount of bosom, and she could have used a hairbrush. The boy toy had a smear of hot-pink lipstick down his cheek.

"You know her?" Lucas asked, glancing at Natasha with some curiosity.

"Not really. We're casual acquaintances. We both write romances, so we run in the same circles." Sort of. Natasha breathed much more rarified air than I. She considered me far beneath her.

"Hmmm. Interesting woman." He was still watching her closely. It was hard to say if it was because he was into her, or because it was like watching a train wreck.

"If you say so," I said dryly. I stared down at my own glass. Empty, darn it.

"I recognize the kid. Kyle something. One of the bartenders here at the resort. Who's the man staring at her like he'd be happy to wring her neck?" Lucas asked.

I glanced across the room where a short, balding man glared at Natasha and her shenanigans. He did, indeed, look like wringing her neck was a real possibility. His raspberry and cream striped shirt clashed with the angry red of his face. "That's Jason Winters. Natasha's almost-ex-husband. The two have a precarious relationship." Which was putting it mildly.

"I see. Well, I shall leave you ladies to enjoy your evening." He gave me a meaningful look. Which caused odd flutters in the region of my stomach. "I look forward to seeing you again, Ms. Roberts."

"Uh, sure. Likewise," I muttered as he strode away, cutting an elegant figure as he made his way through the crowd toward the exit.

"Do you know who that was?" Cheryl hissed, eyes on Lucas's retreating figure. He had a rather nice posterior aspect, not that I noticed. Much.

I shrugged. "Not really."

"Lucas Salvatore is like the number-one best-selling thriller writer. He's been raking in the dough for a dozen years at least. They've made movies of his books. Blockbusters. Like with famous actors."

"Oh. That's nice."

Cheryl rolled her eyes. "Nice? The man is filthy rich. And he was flirting with you."

I gave a snort of disbelief. "Sure he was." And if she believed that, I had an igloo in Arizona to sell her.

# # #

The party was winding down, more than half the attendees having disappeared over the last half hour. Natasha, on the other hand, was still going strong. She was draped over her boy toy, grinding against him with her lower half. It was awkward, to say the least.

"For crying out loud," Cheryl said a little too loudly. She was on her third glass of wine. Wine made Cheryl exceedingly honest. "They should get a room. Give the rest of us a break. I swear my eyeballs are bleeding."

Whipping around like a snake scenting prey, Natasha zeroed in on Cheryl. Oh, great. Just what I needed. Jet lagged, a little tipsy, and definitely not in the mood, I watched Natasha stalk toward my best friend.

"Listen, you little harpy," Natasha started, her medically enhanced features twisted in a drunken sneer.

"Natasha, she didn't mean anything," I said, stepping in front of Cheryl. "We're all tired. It's been a long day. Why don't we go to bed and pick this up in the morning?"

Natasha snorted, looking at Cheryl like she was so much dog poo. "She's just a jealous little witch. Can't get a man. Can't sell books."

"Jealous? Of you?" Cheryl burst out laughing. I could hear the slight edge of hysteria. Natasha was full of it, of course. Cheryl got plenty of male interest, but she was focused on her career. And she did sell books. Scads of them. She just wasn't in Natasha's category. Not many are. Still, Cheryl tended to be sensitive about those subjects. She thrust her chin out. "Oh, yeah, I've always wanted to be a drunken lush."

Natasha let out a scream of rage and charged around me at Cheryl. Cheryl's drink went one way, the glass shattering on the marble tile and red wine splashing across a white tablecloth. Cheryl herself went the other way, Natasha on top her screeching like a banshee. I stood there with my mouth open like an idiot while the two of them rolled around, yelling insults at each other and occasionally landing punches. Cheryl, being less drunk and much younger, was landing better hits, but Natasha was a wily one, and Cheryl would likely be sporting a black eye come morning.

Shaking myself out of my stupor, I reached down and grabbed the nearest arm, trying to yank whomever it belonged to away from the fight. "Stop it. Both of you. For goodness sake— *Ouch!*" I got an elbow in the cheekbone for my trouble. Cheryl wouldn't be the only one with a black eye.

"Here. Let me." It was Lucas, back from wherever he'd slunk off to. He grabbed Natasha under her armpits and lifted her off Cheryl as easily as if he were lifting a child. It couldn't have been as easy as it looked. Natasha was screaming and kicking the entire time.

I leaned over to help Cheryl off the floor, my cheekbone still smarting from whoever's elbow. I was blaming Natasha.

"Ms. Winters, you need to calm down," Lucas was saying in a soothing voice.

Natasha let out a string of words that would have had my mother reaching for the soap.

"Now, is that any way for a lady to talk?" Lucas asked mildly.

My eyes widened. If Lucas Salvatore didn't want a knee to the groin, he probably should back off the lecturing. Let me tell you, if a man spoke to me that way, he'd be missing body parts.

Fortunately for Lucas, Mr. Winters appeared. He somehow got Natasha more or less under control as he guided her out of the ballroom. Her boy toy had long since disappeared. Probably embarrassed to death, or worried about losing his job. I was pretty sure he was one of the bar staff since he wore a staff polo shirt.

With Natasha gone and the fight over, bystanders drifted off either to the bar or their rooms. *Nothing to see here, folks.*

"Can you believe the nerve of that…*woman*?" Cheryl huffed as we exited the ballroom. The way she said the word "woman," I was pretty sure Cheryl had a stronger word in mind. "Jealous? Of *her*? As if! At least I don't need to drape myself all over some kid to get attention."

"Well said," I murmured. I didn't bother pointing out it was Cheryl's loud mouth that started the problem in the first place.

The wide double doors swished open, and we stepped from the frigid air conditioning of the main resort building into the humid heat of the Florida night. The Fairwinds Resort was made of several individual buildings, four of which framed a peaceful central courtyard complete with swaying palm trees, umbrella shaded bistro tables, and a bubbling fountain.

I let out a huge yawn. "Boy, I'm exhausted. I think it's time to hit the hay." I was hoping Cheryl would catch the hint. She did.

"I could use a hot shower," she agreed. "And eight hours of sleep. Classes start tomorrow, and I want to be fresh." She gave me a perky, albeit slightly tipsy, smile.

Since we were housed in separate buildings, she waved goodbye and tottered off across the brick paved courtyard. I sank down on one of the benches lining the walkway. It was well past midnight, but I wasn't ready to go to my room. My blood was still thrumming from the earlier excitement. Hopefully by tomorrow all the gossip would be about Natasha's behavior rather than about Cheryl. Poor thing would be so embarrassed come morning. She was usually so quiet and reserved, but put a few drinks in her and anything could happen.

"You look like you could use a drink."

I glanced up. "Are you following me?"

Lucas's brilliant white smile flashed, and he gave an elegant shrug. I noticed his suit jacket was gone. Likely in deference to the lingering heat of the day. "It's a small resort. I'm buying."

"Well then," I said, standing up and smoothing the skirt of my mint-green sundress, "I'm drinking. Lead on."

The lobby bar was the only place open that late at night. The round bar, ringed by black leather barstools, sat in the center of the hotel lobby, serving coffee in the morning and booze at night. A couple of other NWA members sat chatting over glasses of wine. Either they'd missed the excitement in the ballroom or they didn't care, as neither of them gave us a second look.

The bartender of the evening was a middle-aged man with a buzz cut and a cheerful expression. He was slicing lemons, wielding the very large butcher knife in his hand with the sort of grace I always envied.

"What's your poison?" Lucas asked as the bartender came around to take our orders.

I settled carefully onto the barstool, careful not to tip it over. I was not a small woman, which could make such perches rather treacherous. "Blackberry bourbon, please. On the rocks."

He lifted an eyebrow as if he found my beverage choice interesting, but said nothing. He ordered an Old Fashioned for himself, and we sat in silence, watching the bartender work his magic.

Drinks in hand, Lucas lifted his glass in a toast. "To new friends and interesting times."

"Isn't that a curse?"

He appeared amused. "Only if you want it to be."

I took a thoughtful sip of my bourbon. "I guess time will tell."

I had no idea how prophetic my words would be.

Chapter 2
A Diabolical Discovery

Lucas would have been happy to buy me another drink and continue talking, but I was mere chapters from finishing my latest novel, *The Studly Cowboy's Mail Order Bride*. Dixon and Daphne, the aforementioned cowboy and his bride, were cornered by a gang of notorious outlaws, and Dixon had only two bullets left. All very exciting. I was sure my readers were going to love it.

When I first started writing, I'd decided thrillers were where it was at. Romantic ones, of course, but that was four years before the genre became popular, and my books didn't sell. Plus, I might have had a flair for the melodramatic. Just a touch. After that, I'd tried just about every genre you can imagine: erotic romance, paranormal, contemporary. Nothing worked. And then I tried a historical romance with just a touch of over-the-top drama. It sold like proverbial hotcakes. And the rest, as they say, was history. My rabid readers couldn't get enough of the bodice rippers I gleefully churned out. I love it. They loved it. It was sort of perfect. Sure, people looked down their noses and called my books "trash," but I laughed all the way to the bank.

As I wove my way across the courtyard of the resort, perhaps a tiny bit tipsy from too much blackberry bourbon, my mind was completely focused on the next scene I would write. How was I going to get Dixon and Daphne out of their dreadful situation? I smirked a little as a couple of different options came to mind. Followed, naturally, by Daphne throwing herself at Dixon. I could see it all very clearly in my mind. Talk about steamy. My fingers itched for my keyboard.

Loud voices derailed my train of thought. Frowning, I glanced around the courtyard trying to find the culprits. When I caught sight of the shadowy figures beneath a small cluster of palm trees, I shook my head. Of course, Natasha Winters was right in the thick of it. She was yelling rather drunkenly at what looked like her almost-ex-husband, Jason. It was hard to tell what with the shadows, but he was the right height and build, and he had on the same color shirt I'd seen Jason wearing: that awful striped shirt, which suited his frame and complexion not at all.

"Listen, you nitwit," Natasha snarled. "I am tired of financing you and your little floozy. I'm done."

Oh, juicy. I knew Jason had cheated on Natasha. Everyone in the romance industry did. That was why their marriage broke up. Natasha had gone on a drunken social media rant. There'd even been pictures, though those had been taken down eventually. But plenty of screen shots of her meltdown remained. Most writers would probably end up with their careers in the toilet. Not Natasha. Her sales had skyrocketed. The bigger and crazier her rants, the more people gobbled up her books.

Of course, the ridiculous thing was that Natasha had been cheating on Jason for years. Everyone knew that, too. Or at least everyone who went to writer conventions. Natasha would always end up with some random waiter, bartender, or male stripper for the weekend. Somehow that was okay, but the minute Jason strayed, she was done. Frankly, if I were Jason, I'd have dumped her ages ago. Of course, there was the money to consider. From my understanding, Jason hadn't worked at a regular job in years, thanks to Natasha's income. For a while, that had been fine. Apparently, Natasha finally grew tired of Jason and his girlfriend sponging off of her. Couldn't say I blamed Natasha.

Jason held up his hands, placating. "Listen, Tash—."

"Don't call me that. Don't ever call me that," she shrieked. I wished I could see her face. Still, my imagination sufficed. "Okay, fine. Geez, calm down. You're making a scene." He glanced around, but he didn't see me, secreted as I was behind the corner of my building.

That really got her going. I won't repeat the words that came out of her mouth. Let's just say it would have made a sailor blush.

The gist of it was that Natasha was done paying and Jason was trying to change her mind. Part of me wanted to stay and listen to the argument. Kind of like a rubbernecking at an accident on the freeway. But Dixon and Daphne were calling, and who was I to ignore the call?

The elevator pinged, and the doors slid open. Right before I stepped inside, I heard Jason yell, "You owe me, Natasha. You do this and you'll be sorry."

# # #

My room at the Fairwinds was more of a mini suite. The front room, next to the door, held two double beds with smushy pillow-top mattresses and perfectly pressed white cotton sheets. A short hall—the bathroom just off it—connected the bedroom to the front room. It was a nice bathroom. Nothing fancy, but it did have a rainfall showerhead and a very large tub. I decided I needed one in my own cottage back home. The rainfall showerhead, I mean. I already have a rather nice claw foot tub.

The front room contained a tiny kitchenette and sitting area to the right, and a dining table on the left. The wide glass doors opened up to the most amazing views of white sand beaches, the turquoise Gulf beyond. Breathtaking. And nothing like my own Pacific Ocean back home.

Unlike this stretch of Florida coast, Oregon sand was made of rocks, so it was dark, more tan-colored than white. Except on the sunniest days, the water tended toward a rich, stormy blue-gray. I missed it already. I loved the wildness of that rugged coast.

Still, the Gulf called to me. Suddenly the trials and tribulations of Dixon and Daphne couldn't hold my interest. I needed a walk on that beach. Maybe clear my head a bit. Get over my annoyance with Natasha Winters and her nonsense so I could write.

Closing down my laptop, I threw on a pair of jeans capris, a thin t-shirt, and my flip-flops. I wrapped my long, dark brown hair into a bun—otherwise I'd end up with a rat's nest— and tucked my cell phone in one pocket and my room card in the other. I quickly made my way to the elevator, across the courtyard, and out onto the beach.

The sand glowed softly beneath the nearly full moon, and the sound of the waves drowned out most everything else. They weren't the loud booming crashes of the Pacific, but a softer, slower rush. Soothing.

Between me and the Gulf, rows of beach chairs huddled, dark shapes against the light sand. Two cabanas stood sentinel against the dark sky, their white canvas sides flapping slightly in the light breeze.

A breeze which in no way dispelled the oppressive humidity that lingered. According to the taxi driver on the way in from the airport, there had been a storm a couple days before. He'd assured Cheryl and me that the humidity would lift soon. I wasn't holding my breath.

Wiping a light sheen of sweat from my brow, I strolled slowly across the firm sand, winding my way between the huddled shapes of folded-up lounge chairs. The cabanas were still up, which was unusual this late at night. Apparently whoever was responsible was having a lazy day. As I passed the cabanas, something caught the corner of my eye. With a frown I stopped, turning toward the second cabana. A dark shape was sprawled across the seat. Someone was inside.

I started to turn away, figuring it was a pair of lovers getting romantic in the moonlight. Couldn't say I blamed them, except it was so darn humid the thought of touching another human being made me squidgy. Then I realized the shape wasn't moving. Maybe someone had fallen asleep or passed out. I shook my head. *Not my business.*

But, of course, curiosity had always been my downfall, so I carefully picked my way across the sand and entered the cabana. It was so dark I couldn't make out much of anything other than the person appeared to be a woman. She was on the slender side and wearing one of the white bathrobes the resort passed out to the better-paying guests. Her blond hair spilled across the white fabric of the cabana's seating area as she lay prone on the lounge chair, her face turned slightly toward me, though I couldn't make it out.

"Excuse me." I cleared my throat. The woman didn't move. I tried again. "Hello? Ma'am?" Still not a sound or flicker of movement.

One pale arm dangled from the couch. It was so still. Suddenly I had a really bad feeling.

Swallowing hard, I moved closer and reached down to touch that hand. Cold. Far too cold. Feeling a little queasy, I checked for a pulse like I'd seen people do in the movies. Of course, I had no idea what I was doing, so the action was pointless.

Then I saw it: the handle of a knife sticking out of her back, a dark stain spreading across the white robe. I swallowed hard. I should call the police.

I will, I assured myself. *Just as soon as I see who it is.*

I leaned over until I caught sight of her face. Holy crackers, it was Natasha Winters, and she was stone-cold dead.

Chapter 3
Detective Hottie

A uniformed police officer arrived first at the scene. She was short and stocky with mousy hair slicked back in a tight bun. Her pleasant, but serious, expression never wavered as she confirmed I was the 911 caller, then she ushered me away from the body and quickly set up a perimeter with crime scene tape. Just like in the movies. Then she pulled out a cell phone and began tapping wildly at the keys while keeping a gimlet eye on me.

"You discovered the body?" she asked without preamble, fingers flying over the touch screen. Light glinted off her nametag and badge. It was dark, but it looked like her innocuous last name was "Smith."

I glanced at Natasha's body still lying in the cabana, her blond hair swaying in the slight breeze, the bloodstain locked in my mind forever. Creepy. Something niggled at the corner of my mind. Something about the crime scene. Unfortunately, I couldn't quite grasp it. Shock, maybe.

"Yes. I found the body." What else was there to say?

"Your name and address, please."

"Viola Roberts," I said and then rattled off my home address in Astoria, Oregon. All standard procedure. I knew this from watching true-crime shows on television. The Investigation Discovery Channel was my guilty pleasure. I was particularly enamored of Lt. Joe

Kenda, Homicide Hunter. I'd even gone so far as to buy one of his mugs.

"Walk me through what happened leading to the discovery." Her expression was deadpan. She'd make a great poker player. All business, this one.

I cleared my throat and swiped a thin layer of sweat off my upper lip. It was humid as all get out. I would have liked to take this into the air-conditioned hotel, but I got that she couldn't leave the body unattended.

"I was trying to work, but I couldn't focus, so I decided to take a walk along the beach."

"What do you do for a living?" Officer Smith asked, sounding almost bored. I knew she wasn't. I could see the glint in her eyes that told me she was taking in absolutely everything.

"I'm a writer. I'm here for the conference." I wasn't sure she knew there was a conference at the hotel, but she likely would before the end of the night.

She nodded sharply. "You took a walk."

"Yes. I was headed to the water when I caught sight of Natasha, er, the body out of the corner of my eye. I thought maybe she was passed out or something, so I figured I'd better wake her and get her inside."

"You knew the victim?" Her eyes narrowed in suspicion.

Great. Not only was I probably a suspect since I'd found the body, but the fact I knew her could really get me in hot water.

"I know of her," I corrected. "We run in the same circles. Go to the same conferences. We've met, but nothing more than that. We don't hang out or anything."

"Why? You have a problem with her?" She tapped one blunt finger against her phone screen.

Well, darn. My mother raised me not to lie, but if I admitted what I thought of Natasha, they'd probably throw me in the slammer and toss away the key. Did Florida have the death penalty? I shuddered.

"Not a problem, really. Natasha is, was, just never my sort of person. We're civil, but not BFFs or anything." Which was true. Natasha and I had never gotten into an argument. Her disagreement had been with Cheryl, which I figured Officer Smith didn't need to know since Cheryl wasn't the killer. Of that I was certain. "These conferences attract all sorts of people. You can't be tight with all of them."

"All right," Officer Smith said as the paramedics arrived, followed by two more uniformed officers, some CSIs, and a plainclothes policeman. "Stay here. The detective in charge will likely have some questions for you."

I nodded and sank down onto one of the nearby lounge chairs. Might as well make myself comfortable.

What looked like the head of hotel security and probably the night manager swarmed over the sand to join the plainclothes policeman. Bet he was the detective in charge, if the gold shield was anything to go by. I'd never met a real homicide detective. I couldn't help but feel a little thrill, even as I told myself not to be so macabre, what with Natasha lying dead just a few feet away.

One of the CSIs set up a flood lamp. As he switched it on, I got a good look at the body for the first time. The whole scene looked unreal, the dark stain like something from a movie. And the knife... I froze for a split second. That was what had been niggling at me. The knife was identical to the one the bartender had been using to cut up lemons. Should I mention that to Officer Smith? Surely that would be important. It meant the killer was the bartender. Or one of them, anyway. Didn't it?

I turned to glance at the detective, and my breath caught in my throat. He was young, or at least younger than I was—probably in his mid-thirties— taller than the other men around him and leanly muscled. Or at least he looked that way under the rumpled, cheap suit. His brown hair needed a trim, and he was clutching a large cup of coffee in one nicely shaped hand. The man could have been a movie star, he was that good looking.

And here I sat looking like the victim of a reverse makeover with my makeup washed off and my hair a disaster, thanks to the humidity. My usual glossy waves had turned into a frizzy hot mess. Figured. First really good-looking man I'd come across, and he probably not only thought I was a homeless person, but a murderer to boot.

Of course Lucas Salvatore was a darn fine-looking man, too. Although he didn't have that wonderfully dangerous edge that the detective had. Detective Hottie was one interesting man. I couldn't wait for the interrogation to begin.

# # #

Thirty seconds in and I'd changed my mind. Interrogation wasn't fun, and it had ceased to be interesting fifteen minutes ago. Detective Hottie was a jerk. I tried really hard not to glare at him. I doubted I was successful.

"Giving me dirty looks isn't going to help you, Ms. Roberts," he said sternly. I usually thought of hazel eyes as being warm, but his were icy and cold. "I'm just doing my job."

I sighed. It was true. "Sorry, what was it you asked, Detective...?"

"Detective Diego Costa, ma'am."

I wished he'd stop calling me "ma'am." It made me feel ancient. "I'm not that old," I muttered under my breath."

"Excuse me, ma'am?"

I barely resisted the urge to growl. "Nothing, Detective."

He gave me a blank look that was downright scary. "When was the last time you saw the victim alive?"

"Like I told Officer Smith, Natasha Winters was alive and well at about ten p.m. I saw her in the courtyard arguing with her almost-ex-husband, Jason Winters."

"*Almost* ex-husband?"

"It's a long story."

He stared at me with those scary eyes. "I've got time."

"Most of what I know is only third-party gossip, mind you."

"Understood."

"Fine," I agreed. "When Natasha first started making money as a writer, she hired a personal assistant, Piper Ross. Piper was young, good looking, and...well, one thing led to another."

"I see." There was zero expression in Costa's voice. I had no idea if he approved, disapproved, or plain didn't care.

"Basically, word is that Jason and Piper had an affair, so Natasha fired Piper, threw Jason out on his, er, backside, and filed for divorce. They've been fighting nonstop over the money and the divorce still isn't final."

"No pre-nup then?"

I shrugged. "Wouldn't think so. Natasha and Jason were married for something like twenty years before Natasha hit it big. Until then it was Jason supporting them."

"I'll check on that," Costa assured me. "The fight. What was it about?"

I relayed what I'd heard, knowing the almost-ex-husband would be suspect *numero uno*. I felt bad for Jason. He didn't seem like a killer, but he had been the last person to see Natasha alive. Probably. Still, I couldn't see him committing cold-blooded murder. Or hot-blooded murder, for that matter. He was just so...mild. There was always the possibility that after their argument, Natasha had met up with someone else who had it in for her.

Wow, that really narrows it down, I thought wryly. Half the convention had it in for Natasha. Probably half the hotel staff, too, by now.

After a few more questions, Detective Hottie, I mean Costa, gave me a stern look. The kind meant to make suspects quail in their boots…or flip-flops. I bet he practiced it in the mirror. "That's all for now, ma'am." Ugh. There was that foul word again. "You can go back to your room, but please don't leave the island."

Which meant I was a suspect. Goodie. Of course, since I'd found the body, I wasn't terribly surprised.

"Of course not," I said, giving him a guileless smile. "Wouldn't dream of it. Have a good evening, Detective." And with that, I strode across the smooth, white sand, putting a little extra sway in my hips. If I thought that would distract Detective Costa, I was bound for disappointment. A quick glance over my shoulder told me he was completely focused on the crime scene. He hadn't even given me a second glance. *More's the pity.*

My natural curiosity got the better of me, and with the detective focused elsewhere, I slid behind the first cabana that was a few feet away from the one housing Natasha's body. Huddled behind the billowing white canvas, I attempted to eavesdrop. I'd seen Jessica Fletcher do it plenty of times. Surely I was smart enough to pull it off. Maybe I could learn something. After all, Cheryl would want all the details, and I couldn't disappoint. Not to mention, with myself as one of the prime suspects, I felt the need to clear my name as soon as possible. Couldn't do that unless I knew what was going on, now, could I?

Costa's voice was a low rumble against the background of wind and waves. I tucked a strand of errant hair behind my ear, as if that could help me hear better. He was talking to Smith. No doubt getting her recorded version of events. She'd been first on the scene, and I knew from my crime shows, that meant her observations would be important to the lead detective. I wondered what she was saying about me. I couldn't make out their conversation.

Frustrated, I finally gave up, right about the time the coroner prepared to load the body on a gurney. I really didn't want to stick around to watch them haul Natasha away. The thought of her lying dead squidged me out. Even more, I didn't need Detective Costa catching me lurking around the crime scene. No doubt I'd go to the top of his suspect list pronto.

With a quick glance to make sure no one was watching, I slipped through the shadows toward the pool. My bare foot hit something hard, sending the small object skittering across the sand. With a frown, I leaned over to pick it up. It was a simple, narrow, silver bracelet. The adjustable kind. It looked like maybe there was something etched on it, but the light was poor. I thought for a split second about turning it over to Costa, then hesitated. The bracelet might have nothing to do with the murder. It was nowhere near the body, after all. Plenty of people played on the beach every day. It could belong to anyone. I'd do a little research on it. If I couldn't find the owner, well, then I would think about turning it over to Costa.

Mind made up, I tucked the bracelet into my capris pocket and hurried across the sand toward the resort. Circling the pool, I huddled against the side of one of the buildings as the coroner passed by with his burden, then slipped down the passageway toward my building. I didn't relax until I was inside my room with the door locked and bolted.

Chapter 4
The Mystery of 415

Violent pounding startled me from a dead sleep. I sat bolt upright in bed, hair half covering my face. Flailing wildly, I managed something resembling, "Wha... Where... Who... Ack!" That last one was shrieked as I hit the floor with a resounding *thump*.

I grimaced. Maybe I shouldn't use the word "dead" quite so freely. There was way too much of that going on already.

From my position on the floor between the two beds, I squinted at the clock. Three a.m. Who on earth would be banging on the door at this hour? Grabbing my robe off the other bed, I staggered to my feet and wobbled my way to the door. Peeking through the peephole, it was hard to make out the other person in the dim light, but I recognized her form immediately: Cheryl. Whatever was going on, it couldn't be any good to drag Cheryl out of bed at this ungodly hour.

Flipping back the deadbolt, I threw open the door. "What on earth...?"

Cheryl didn't give me a chance to say another word. She launched herself at me, nearly taking both of us to the floor. I staggered back, letting the door slam shut. She was babbling incoherently and sobbing so hard, I was half afraid she'd break a rib. Mine or hers. Could go either way.

Cheryl is a slender woman. Tiny even. Not at all like my robust self. It would take quite a bit to snap anything of mine.

I patted her back. She was wearing a fuschia silk robe with giant blue flowers, and it was slippery under my fingers. "There, there." I felt like an idiot, but wasn't that what people said to comfort the distraught? "The big, bad bogeyman is gone. You're safe."

She pulled back, giving me a wide-eyed stare. She'd obviously fallen asleep with her makeup on because the remnants of mascara gave her raccoon eyes. On her, it was kind of adorable. "No, he's not!" she gasped.

"What?"

"The bogeyman is in my room."

I gave her a look. "Did you have another nightmare?"

Like most writers, Cheryl was prone to some rather creative dreaming. One time she'd dreamed that it was Thanksgiving and she'd forgotten to bake pie. So, she got up at four in the morning and started baking a pumpkin pie. Frankly, it'd been a win for me since I got to eat it. Another time she called me scared to death that she'd been kidnapped by aliens. In her defense, she was still half asleep when she called. She was embarrassed to death when she finally woke up fully and realized what she'd done.

"No. I swear. His name is Detective Coaster." She frowned. "No, that's not right."

"Costa?" I asked suspiciously.

"Oh, yes. That's it. How'd you know?"

"Come sit down. Tell me about it." I dragged her into the living room and pushed her onto the couch. Normally I would never buy anything from the mini bar, but these were extenuating circumstances. I snagged a mini bottle of tequila for Cheryl and a whiskey for me. I prefer bourbon or brandy, but desperate times…

I twisted off the cap and handed her the tequila. "Drink."

She frowned. "Don't you have any fruit juice?"

"Fresh out. Down it fast. That's my motto."

She tossed it back in one gulp, making faces at the burn, while I joined her on the couch, sipping a little more delicately. "Okay, tell me what happened," I demanded.

Cheryl took a shuddering breath. "I was asleep. You know, totally out of it. And there was this knock at the door. It was the police." Her eyes were a little too wide. I handed her the remaining half of my whiskey, which she downed like a champ. "Like the actual police. With badges and guns and everything."

"Yes. I'm familiar," I said dryly.

"This detective was there. Costas."

"Costa. What did he want?"

"I don't know!" she wailed, fingers twisting around the empty whiskey bottle. "He just kept asking me all these questions about Natasha Winters and our kerfuffle." Only Cheryl would call a knock-down, drag-out catfight a kerfuffle.

"Go on."

"He was acting really weird. Like he thought I did something bad. Then he told me not to leave town or he'd arrest me," she wailed.

My eyes really narrowed at that. "Did he tell you Natasha is dead?"

Cheryl tried to take another drink from the bottle and frowned when she realized it was empty. "What?" she asked, only half listening.

"Natasha is dead, Cheryl."

She turned white. "Dead?" she whispered. "How did she die?"

"Knife in the back. Literally."

"It was murder? N-no. He didn't say anything about that. Oh my goodness. He thinks I did it, doesn't he?" Cheryl was no dummy, which was one of the reasons we were friends.

I nodded. "I'm thinking he's definitely got you on his suspect list. You're in good company. I'm on there, too."

"Why? You didn't get in a fight with her."

"Nope. I found her body."

Cheryl's mouth dropped open. She forgot her upset in the face of such scintillating gossip. "What? Tell me everything!"

I gave her a quick rundown on my rather grisly discovery, followed by my equally grisly interrogation by Detective Costa. "I'm right at the top of his suspect list. Along with Jason, of course."

"And me," Cheryl said mournfully. "I can't believe you discovered her body. How awful."

"It wasn't that bad."

She gave me a look.

"Okay, it was bad, but I didn't see much. Touching her was the worst."

"Ew! Why on earth did you touch her?"

"To check for a pulse, of course." I then told her about the bracelet.

"You didn't turn it over? Isn't that withholding evidence?" she asked.

"Only if it *is* evidence. It could be nothing. Don't worry. I'm going to do a little digging and if it turns out it's important, I'll fork it over."

Cheryl sat back with a sad look. "You're so much braver than I am, Viola. I don't know what I'm going to do. How am I going to tell my mother I'm a murder suspect?"

"Don't worry." I patted her knee. "I'm going to prove once and for all that neither of us murdered Natasha Winters."

"How are you going to do that?"

I smiled. "I'm going to find the real killer."

# # #

"I can't believe we're doing this," Cheryl hissed in my ear. She was dressed in black from head to toe. Even her flip-flops were black. Which was unnecessary since it was broad daylight, but she'd insisted on dressing the part. I never heard of a cat burglar in flip-flops.

"*We're* not doing this. I am. You're standing guard, remember?" It was early the morning after I'd found Natasha's body, and we were huddled outside her room just beyond sight of the housekeeping cart. It was piled high with clean towels, rolls of toilet paper, and an assortment of cleaning products. The maid was inside room 410, just a few doors down from Natasha's room, number 415.

"How are we going to get the key?" Cheryl whispered.

"We're not. I'm going to get housekeeping to let me in."

She shot me a look of disbelief. "She's never going to do that. Look at all the crime scene tape. No way is she going to let you waltz in there."

"You just watch. And stay out of sight."

She nodded, clearly happy to not be part of the breaking and entering. Well, technically it was only "entering," since I was going to get in using a key. Totally legit. Well, semi-legit, anyway.

I dashed across the hallway to room 415 and ripped the crime scene tape away from the door. Wadding it into a ball, I stuffed it into the nearest trashcan before dusting off my hands. Straightening my shoulders, I made my way casually toward room 410 and the housekeeping cart.

It would have been so perfect if the housekeeper had just left her key card on the cart. But, of course, that would have been too easy. I peeked into the room to find a small, round woman with graying hair in a thick braid down her back. She was in the middle of remaking the bed, her movements quick and efficient. Around her left wrist was a purple wristband, and from it hung a key card. Now the question was how to convince her to open Natasha's room for me. If I was lucky, she'd never actually seen Natasha. After all, we'd only been here a couple days.

I knocked loudly on the open door, and the woman started, whirling to face me. She had a wide face and soft, brown eyes. I hoped her temperament was as sweet as her expression.

"Excuse me," I said, giving her a friendly smile. "I seem to have locked myself out of my room with my keycard inside. Could you let me in?"

She frowned in confusion and said something in Spanish. I frowned, too—my Spanish was more than a little rusty. No way could I rephrase what I'd just said in that language. So, I tried again—in English—adding a few hand gestures to get my point across. Her expression cleared, and she bobbed her head in agreement as I motioned her down the hall to Natasha's room.

Either she hadn't seen Natasha before or she didn't care, because she let me in the room, no problem. I thanked her in Spanish, which was about all of the language I knew, and she gave me a wide smile before disappearing back down the hall into room 410.

I waved Cheryl over. "Okay, the plan. You stand guard. If the cops show up, text me."

"Why would the cops show up? Haven't they already been here?" she asked, peering into the darkened interior of the hotel room.

"Of course. But they might have to come back."

Cheryl's eyes narrowed. "Wouldn't they notice their tape was missing?"

Good point. "Sure. But they won't know who took it down."

"Unless they dust for fingerprints."

I rolled my eyes. "Stop being so logical. Just stand guard while I check out Natasha's room. They could have missed something important." They did on *Murder, She Wrote*. Jessica Fletcher would always find the clue, and it would be the key to solving the case.

Probably getting my investigative know-how from a television show wasn't the best thing in the world, but it was what I had to work with. No way was I letting Detective Hottie lock Cheryl or me up because he was too busy pointing the finger at us instead of hunting the real culprit.

Cheryl hurried back to her hiding place and gave me the thumbs-up. I nodded and entered the room, letting the door close softly behind me. I didn't throw the deadbolt just in case I had to leave quickly.

Natasha's room was identical to mine: two rooms connected by a hallway. The first room contained two double beds, just like mine, and the front room had a wide slider door facing the ocean, just like mine. It even had the same gold faux-silk curtains. The only real difference was that the rooms were a little bigger, and there was a very narrow balcony off the slider. Just wide enough for a miniscule bistro table and two ornate wrought-iron chairs. My room only had a Juliette balcony. Which was fine. The weather was too humid to leave the slider open anyway, and I'd just as soon enjoy my morning coffee in the comfort of air-conditioning rather than the glaring sun.

The beds were neatly made. Apparently Natasha didn't make it back to her room before she was killed. Or, at least, she didn't make it to bed. The wooden nightstand in between the two beds held a collection of hand creams, throat lozenges, and a stack of paperbacks, all romances. Apparently Natasha hadn't graduated to e-readers like the rest of us. I perused the titles but found nothing of interest. I'd either read them already, or they weren't my thing. Not that I planned on stealing from a dead woman, mind you. Not unless it was absolutely essential to the investigation.

The closet contained nine pairs of shoes. Most of them sandals with varying heel heights and levels of sparkle. Several dresses hung neatly from their hangers, and three empty suitcases were tucked back in the corner. I winced at the thought of how much she'd spent on checked luggage, but I guess you can do that when you make seven figures.

In the upper corner of the closet, the small safe stood open and empty. I had no idea if the police had opened it and taken whatever was inside, or if Natasha simply hadn't used it.

Moving to the dresser, I pulled open one drawer at a time. More clothes. Enough underwear to open a lingerie store. All of it lacey and fussy. Exactly what I would have expected of a woman like Natasha Winters. Personally, I preferred comfort. Which, I supposed, could partially explain why I was still single at over forty. I just didn't see the point in having a skinny piece of satin wedged up my backside.

I took the bathroom next. Again, nothing but the usual makeup and bath stuff. Clean towels hung neatly from the racks, looking as if they'd never been used, and the toilet paper rolls had neat little triangles still folded on the ends. It was looking more and more like Natasha hadn't come back to her room all day; if she had, I suspected at least the triangles would be gone.

I inspected the living room and kitchen area last. Like my own dining room table, Natasha's contained her laptop cord—the police likely took the laptop itself—and various papers and pens. In the kitchenette, I found an open bag of expensive coffee, a bunch of bananas, and an unopened bottle of red wine. The fridge held coffee creamer and six single-serving containers of Greek yogurt, all vanilla.

Through the sliding glass door, I could see a view of the Gulf. It was, in a word, stunning. The one thing about Florida I truly liked. Off to the side, cabanas stood sentinel over early morning beachgoers. The one where Natasha's body had been found was still wrapped in yellow crime scene tape.

With a sigh, I started for the door. There was nothing in the suite to indicate what Natasha had been up to or why someone might have killed her. I was halfway to the door when a thought struck me. I turned around and headed for the phone sitting neatly on the end table next to the couch. Beside it was a cheap pen and a pad of paper with the hotel's logo on the top. I picked up the pad and tilted it toward the light. Sure enough, something had been written there. I could only assume it had been written by Natasha since, from what I could tell of my own room, the pads were replaced with each new guest.

I ripped off the top sheet and tucked it into my capris pocket. I could figure out what was written on it later. As I headed toward the door, my phone vibrated in my pocket. I pulled it out. It was a text from Cheryl.

Police coming! GET OUT!!

Chapter 5
Adventures in Sleuthing

I ran for the door, my flip-flops making an awkward *splooch* sound on the marble floor. My hand was on the door handle when a second text came in. A quick glance at the screen and I froze in place.

Too late! HIDE!!

Cheryl was overly fond of exclamation marks. I gritted my teeth, desperately looking for a place to hide. The closet was a no-go. They could easily open it and find me. Ditto the bathroom. I considered the balcony, but tossed that aside. Even if I closed the drapes, they could open them easily enough and see me. And I wasn't exactly built for climbing over balconies. Even if I managed, with my luck I'd get locked out.

That left one place: under one of the beds. I eyed the narrow openings with a malevolent eye. I loathed tight spaces, and these barely looked high enough for a mouse to crawl under, never mind my generous backside. Nothing for it. I'd have to put on my big-girl panties, suck it up, and squeeze under.

Crossing my fingers, I dropped to my belly and wriggled beneath the bed nearest the door. My butt scraped uncomfortably against the wooden slats of the bed frame. My boobs mashed into the floor in a way that told me I was going to be sore later. No doubt my purple t-shirt was covered in dust bunnies. My feet were barely out of sight when the door swung open and a pair of white sneakers entered the room, followed by a pair of scuffed black dress shoes.

I narrowed my eyes. I'd know those shoes anywhere. They went along with the rumpled suit and the scruffy day-old beard growth. Detective Costa. What was he doing here? Well, obviously investigating a murder, but why was he back in Natasha's room when presumably he'd already gone over it last night?

"Thank you, Alfonse," the detective said in his smooth baritone with just a touch of an accent. Barely noticeable, but definitely there. And definitely sexy. I gave myself a mental shake. Costa was the enemy. Well, maybe not enemy, per se, but he was definitely not on my side at the moment.

"*No problemo*, detective," the man called Alfonse replied. I was guessing he was some sort of resort employee. "You want me to wait?"

"I'll be fine on my own."

"Sure thing." The white sneakers passed in front of my hiding place. The heavy fire door opened and slammed shut behind Alfonse. There was a pause. One of those "pregnant" ones.

"You can come out now."

What the—? I closed my eyes and drew in a deep breath. When I opened them I could see the black dress shoes standing right in front of my hiding spot. Was Costa psychic?

I held my breath. Maybe he was just guessing, and if I stayed still, he'd go away.

"I'm not going away."

42

For crying out loud. Was he a mind reader now? With a heavy sigh, I wriggled my way out from under the bed, the metal side rails scraping along my ribs in a most uncomfortable way. Likely I'd have bruises.

Surprisingly, Costa did the gentlemanly thing and reached down to help me to my feet. Unsurprisingly, he gave me a cold, hard, cop stare while he did it.

"Ms. Roberts. Fancy meeting you here." He waited, clearly looking for an answer as to what I was doing in a dead woman's room. A woman whose body I'd discovered only a few hours earlier.

I knew from my crime shows that guilty people babbled nervously, and even though I was nervous as all get out, no way was I going to babble. Nope. I was going to be cool as a cucumber.

"Oh, I was just, you know, passing by. Door was open. Probably the cleaning people? Anyway, I was curious, you know. I've never seen a dead body before. Certainly not a murdered one. We writers are a...curious lot. Thought I'd, um, see where it happened. Well, not "it," per se, since she probably got killed on the beach, right? But, you know, the place she lived, er, stayed..." I trailed off as Costa's expression never changed. So much for not babbling. Nerves. They always got to me.

"Curious, huh?"

"Oh, um, yes. Very. Writer thing. You know." *Shut up. Shut up. Shut up.*

"Yes, you said that already." He gave me a look that said he didn't quite believe me. Probably he could arrest me for contaminating the crime scene or interfering with a murder investigation or something. "You know I could arrest you for interfering with a homicide investigation."

The man really was a mind reader.

"I'm really sorry. I didn't mean to. I won't do it again. I didn't touch anything. Promise," I blathered like a lunatic. "Well, except the door handle, of course. And the slider door. I wanted to see how much better her balcony was." *Oh, good way to incriminate yourself, Viola. Let him know you were jealous of her balcony.* Which I wasn't. Much.

"I suppose the crime scene tape disappeared by itself."

"Uhh, well, no. I took that down myself," I admitted. I was in for it now.

"Hmm." That one sound held a wealth of meaning. None of it boded well for me.

"I promise, if you let me go, I'll never enter this room again." I figured it was a promise I could keep since the only clue I'd found was now residing in my pocket. I probably should give it to Costa, but now that he'd caught me in Natasha's room, I'd likely just moved right to the top of his suspect list. I had even more of a reason to solve her murder now and even less of a reason to show him what I'd found. He'd probably think I planted it.

Costa paused for the longest time. Long enough to leave me squirming. "I'll let you off with a warning this time. But, Ms. Roberts, stay out of my investigation." He had no need to spell it out. The underlying threat was clear.

"Sure thing, detective," I agreed and slipped out the door before he could change his mind.

# # #

"I knew this was a horrible idea," Cheryl wailed over her cheeseburger. "That detective has it in for you now." The breeze off the ocean ruffled her hair. The Flying Fish Grill had wide windows that were always left open to the sea air. It was one of my favorite eating spots on the resort grounds. It was great for people-watching, too.

"It'll be fine," I assured her around a mouthful of grilled chicken and avocado sandwich. A blob of mustard oozed out the other end and plopped on my blue blouse. I sighed as I dabbed it off. Par for the course. The curse of large bosoms. "Sure, Costa's probably more suspicious of me than ever, but I am going to prove to him that neither of us are killers."

Cheryl's brown eyes widened. "What?" she all but shrieked as she dropped her burger back into its basket, sending ketchup droplets shooting across the table. None of them ended up on her. Charmed, that one. "I thought you promised to stay out of the investigation."

"I had my fingers crossed," I said smugly.

Cheryl let out a strangled sound and buried her face in her hands. "Oh, sweet heaven above. This is a horrible idea, Viola. You're bound to get yourself killed or wind up in jail or something."

I waved that off like the nonsense it was. Whoever had killed Natasha had no reason to kill me. Unless I discovered their identity and turned them into the police, of course, but I'd cross that bridge when I came to it. As for ending up in jail, that was a real possibility, but only if I didn't prove my innocence first.

"Look," I said, "I found this in Natasha's room. It looks like she wrote something on it. Maybe it's important." I slid the piece of notebook paper across the table. Cheryl snatched it up and held it to the light with a frown.

"You can't read anything. The impressions are too faint."

"Right, which is why I need a pencil."

She opened her mouth, but before she could respond, a shadow fell across the table. I glanced up to see Lucas Salvatore. His white linen shirt looked crisp and clean against his tanned skin. His hair was perfect, not a strand out of place. Unlike mine. Between the wind and the humidity, I was beginning to look like the victim of a lightning strike. Why did he have to look so perfectly yummy, darn him?

"Good afternoon, ladies. May I join you?"

I opened my mouth to tell him to go away. I didn't need Lucas getting involved in my little plans, but before I could say a thing Cheryl batted her eyelashes and purred, "But of course. Please have a seat."

The metal chair legs scraped softly against the tile as he made himself comfortable. "Now, what was it about needing a pencil?" he asked.

"Viola found a clue. To Natasha's death," Cheryl blurted, picking up her burger again.

I glared at her. The woman hadn't an inkling how to keep a secret. "Cheryl, that's on the down low."

"Don't worry," Lucas said, giving me a meaningful look. "I can keep a secret."

Oh, I just bet you can. "Still, you don't want to get messed up in this."

"Sure, I do," he said warmly. "Anything I can do to help, I'll do it."

I studied him for a moment, wondering what his angle was. Why was he so keen to help? *Oh, my word, maybe he's the killer!*

Of course, that was ridiculous. Why would Lucas Salvatore, a man who could buy and sell Natasha Winters ten times over, want to kill her? Okay, she was a nasty piece of work, but I couldn't see Lucas caring about that. He seemed so...unruffled about darn near everything. As far as I knew, Natasha and Lucas ran in completely different circles. In fact, during the scuffle at the opening night party, they both had acted like they'd never seen each other before. Granted, it was easy enough to pretend not to know each other. What if they'd been lovers who had a falling out, and Lucas killed her in a fit of passion?

No. I couldn't quite see that. For one thing, Natasha was a bit trampy for a class act like Lucas Salvatore, but even if he'd been into her, he was far too old. Natasha liked them young. Lucas was a good-looking guy and in remarkable shape, but he hadn't seen twenty in quite some time.

Once I'd settled in my own mind that Lucas wasn't a true suspect, I decided I could use his help. After all, he was a thriller writer. He must have picked up a thing or two while researching his novels. After all, I'd learned to make pemmican for one of mine. Believe me, that is not something you want to get into.

"All right, this is why I need a pencil," I said, pulling out the slip of paper. "I found this in Natasha's room."

"You broke into a crime scene?" He didn't seem particularly shocked.

"I know right? She's a lunatic," Cheryl muttered.

"Not a crime scene, exactly," I said. "I mean she didn't die there." He gave me a look which I ignored. "In any case," I continued, "if I rub the pencil over the impressions on this sheet of paper, we can read what was written on the pad. It might lead us to the killer."

"Or it might be a shopping list," he pointed out with annoying logic. Cheryl stifled a giggle.

"Do you or do you not have a pencil?" I snapped.

"I do not, I'm afraid, but I am certain I can acquire one." He stood up and strolled to the bar. As he leaned over, his shirt rode up enough that I could see he had a very nice backside. I told myself not to stare.

"Don't you just love how take-charge he is?" Cheryl asked dreamily, swirling a fry around in a pool of ketchup.

"Yeah. Totally. Why did you have to go blab?"

"Because he's an expert."

"He's a *writer*," I snorted, "that doesn't make him an expert on anything except maybe comma usage, and even that's doubtful." Most writers, including yours truly, have a dickens of a time with commas. Thank goodness for line editors, that's all I've got to say.

Editors. Now there was a thought.

"What about Natasha's editor?" I asked.

"Yvonne?" Cheryl frowned. "What about her?"

Yvonne Kittering had been Natasha's acquisitions editor at Romantic Press. Sort of like her rep or sales agent, I guessed—unlike most of us who were published there, who were pretty much left to our own devices and never heard from our acquisitions agents again, Yvonne's sole job was to keep Natasha happy. Not exactly my idea of a dream job. Rumor had it that Yvonne hated Natasha, though I'd never seen Yvonne do anything but suck up.

"Maybe they had a falling out or something. Natasha was notoriously hard to work with," I suggested. "If I were Yvonne, I'd have murdered Natasha years ago."

Cheryl waved that away. "I saw them at the party. They seemed perfectly fine. Yvonne was kissing her backside as usual, and Natasha was lapping it up like she was the Queen of Sheba."

"Huh. Still, I'd like to talk to Yvonne. Even if she isn't a suspect, I bet she would have a good idea on who'd have it in for Natasha. And why."

Lucas returned to the table before I could continue my train of thought, stubby pencil in hand. "As my lady wishes," he said, handing it to me with a flourish.

"Thanks," I said lamely. Laying the paper on the table, I used the broad side of the lead to lightly color over the impressions. Letters became visible, and I frowned.

Cheryl leaned over my shoulder. "What is that? Letters?"

"Yes. Looks like a K and a V. Followed by a number: 506."

"Sounds like a hotel room," Lucas drawled, leaning back in his chair.

It sure did. "Okay, but what about the letters?"

"Maybe they stand for the name of a hotel or something," Cheryl suggested.

"Wait, there's more," I said as I scribbled across the lower half of the paper. "It's a time. Ten p.m. No date, unfortunately, but it couldn't have been too long ago or someone probably would have written over it by now."

"All right," Lucas said, leaning forward and clasping his hands on the table. "We've got a time, a location—I'm betting that room is in this hotel—so what do the letters mean?"

He was right. Natasha wasn't exactly the sort to put herself out, and she didn't much care about being subtle. She'd probably insist the meeting take place as close to her own room as possible. "I'm guessing it was whomever she was meeting."

"KV," Cheryl muttered. "I don't know. That doesn't sound familiar."

I grinned as a thought struck. "Sure it does."

The other two turned expectant gazes in my direction.

"It does?" Cheryl asked.

"Sure. I'll bet you anything it's Kyle. Natasha's boy toy."

Chapter 6
Prime Suspect

Finding Kyle was easy enough. He was ensconced behind the circular bar in the middle of the hotel lobby wearing his hotel uniform of khakis and a white button-down shirt with the Fairwinds Resort logo. The bleached tips of his hair were spiked with gel, and he had one of those golden tans that meant he spent a lot of time in the sun. He was undeniably handsome in a young boy sort of way.

Kyle gave me a friendly, but bland smile as I approached the bar. The kind of smile that tricked a girl into believing she was special, when actually the smile was totally impersonal. I'd seen that look on bartenders and wait staff the world over. I imagined it was a defense mechanism against the unwashed masses.

"Hi, Kyle," I said cheerfully as I slid onto one of the barstools. "Why don't you pour me a nice blackberry bourbon? On the rocks." It was barely past lunchtime, but what the heck…I was on vacation. Sort of.

"Sure thing, ma'am."

I tried not to glare at the "ma'am" comment. "Heh, careful with the 'ma'am' there, Kyle. I'm not that much older than you." I laughed awkwardly.

He gave me a look that told me exactly what he thought of that statement. "Of course...*miss*."

I went ahead and gave him a black scowl. He wasn't looking anyway. "Alrighty then," I said with another awkward laugh. Interrogating people wasn't as easy as Detective Costa made it look. "Hey, you're last name wouldn't happy to be…" I pulled out a random name, "Blackburn, would it?"

He gave me a funny look. "No, it's Vaughn. Why?"

Aha! I'd been right! But I kept my expression bland and gave an airy wave. "Oh, it's silly, but a friend of mine has a cousin named Kyle that works somewhere around here. Wondered if you might be him."

"Nope," he said, pulling a glass from under the counter.

"So, you must have heard about that woman they found dead on the beach."

There was only the slightest pause as he dumped ice into the glass. Then he shrugged. "Sure. Who hasn't?" He splashed brown liquid into the glass and handed it to me. "Seven dollars."

I gave him my room number so he could put it on my tab and took a sip to brace myself. Delicious. "Weren't you dancing with her at the party the night she died?" I asked, all innocent-like. I might have even batted my lashes. I'm not above such things when strictly necessary.

He hesitated as if not sure how to answer. Then he shrugged. "Sure. I was dancing with her. What of it? Not like I saw her after that."

I leaned forward and lowered my voice conspiratorially. "I was just wondering, you know, because they say her husband did it."

That seemed to put him at ease. He gave me another one of those wide, semi-flirtatious smiles that was probably more about tips than anything. "Oh, really?"

"Yeah. So I was wondering if you, you know, saw them together or something. I mean, you could have witnessed something important. Have the police talked to you?"

He leaned forward and lowered his own voice. "Yeah. Someone spilled the beans I was dancing with Natasha that night, so of course they questioned me. But I didn't see anything. After she got in a fight with that skinny chick, I booked." I could only assume that by "skinny chick" he meant Cheryl, who wasn't exactly what I'd call skinny. More slender. "Don't need that kind of negative attention, you know. I wasn't exactly supposed to be at that party, if you know what I mean." He straightened up and started wiping down the bar with a white towel.

I did know what he meant. I doubted fraternizing with guests was something the resort approved of, and I was pretty sure Kyle's activities with Natasha went far beyond a couple dances at a party.

"You know," I said conspiratorially, tapping one fingernail on the edge of my glass, "just between you and me, the police apparently found a note in her room. Something about a meeting that night."

He shrugged. "So whoever she met killed her."

"I imagine so," I said with a knowing nod and a raised brow.

"What did the note say?" he asked, feigning mild disinterest, but I could see he was hanging on to every word.

"I don't know the details, but I do know there was a time and location. One of the empty rooms, I think. I imagine the police will be checking it out. Doing that CSI thing."

He stiffened at that. "Nothing else? On the note, I mean."

I held back a smile. I casually swirled my drink, the ice clinking against the side of the glass. "Well, I think there was a name. At least, that's what I heard." I leaned forward and winked. "But you never know. Police like to hold things back. Smoke out the guilty party. Am I right?"

Was it my imagination, or did he go a bit pale under his tan? He wiped the bar almost obsessively, over and over as if trying to rub out a stain. "You hear the name?"

I sighed. "No. I wish. I'm dying of curiosity. Aren't you?"

He shrugged. "Not my business. Listen, it was nice talking to you, but I gotta get back to work."

"Sure, sure. No worries. One thing before you go, though," I said as a thought struck me. Kyle probably knew a lot of people at the resort. Maybe he'd recognize the bracelet. I pulled the silver bangle out of my handbag and held it up. "Do you recognize this? Maybe it belongs to somebody who works here?" Was it me? Or was that a glimmer of recognition?

Kyle eyed it with disinterest. "Nope. 'Fraid not. Where'd you find it?"

"On the beach last night."

"Really? Huh. Well, you should turn it into Lost and Found."

"Sure, I'll do that," I said, tucking the bracelet back into my pocket. "Sorry to disturb you. I've got a class to get to." I waved him off airily as I downed the last swallow of bourbon. I slid from the stool and walked slowly away from the bar toward the automatic doors leading to the courtyard. I dashed to the side and took up a seat at one of the umbrella-covered tables, sliding a pair of oversized sunglasses on my face. Not much of a disguise, but I doubted Kyle would be looking for me.

I sent Cheryl a quick text to tell her what I was up to. Her response came almost immediately and questioned my sanity while ordering me to remain where I was. She was on her way. I thought about texting Lucas. Having someone with muscles along could come in handy. Then I nixed the idea. Granted, he was in on the investigation, but I still wasn't sure I could trust him entirely. What if he blabbed to the cops or something?

Cheryl still hadn't arrived when Kyle exited the building, a key card clutched tightly in his hand. He didn't see me, just kept his focus straight ahead, a determined expression on his face.

When he was halfway across the courtyard, I got up and followed him. What I wouldn't give for a scarf or a big floppy hat. A disguise.

He got on the elevator, and I watched it slide upward. I'd no doubt he was headed for the fifth floor.

I dashed down the open-air hall and took the stairs as fast as my legs would take me. By the third floor, I was out of breath. By the fourth floor, my legs were rubber. By the time I hit the fifth floor, there was a stitch in my side so bad I was nearly doubled over. This investigation thing was a lot more physically involved than I'd imagined. Maybe I should start working out?

Panting for breath and clinging to the handrail for dear life, I made my way down the walkway toward room 506. The door was held open a few inches by the deadbolt, and I could hear footsteps inside. Yep, Kyle was definitely in there.

Now what? I fidgeted, not sure what to do. *What would Jessica Fletcher do? She'd march right in there and confront him, that's what. Or she'd sneak in and see what he was doing then confront him later. Yeah, great idea.*

I sent Cheryl another quick text to let her know where I was and what I was doing—no sense being stupid about it—then turned my phone on silent. Carefully edging open the door, I slipped inside and let it close softly behind me. I could hear Kyle moving around in the front room. What on earth was he doing in there? Sounded like moving furniture.

I crept to the end of the hall and peered around the corner. Sure enough, Kyle was shoving the couch back against the wall. Clearly he'd been searching for something under or behind the couch. Whatever it was, it didn't look like he'd found it, if the frown on his face was anything to go by.

The lamp beside the couch lit the room only dimly. The curtains were drawn tight so not a drop of sunshine slipped in. It was odd, though. I was sure the curtains had been open earlier that day. Had the maid closed them? Or had Kyle?

Kyle made a growl of frustration and kicked the couch viciously. He ran a hand through his hair, mussing up the blond strands, before turning toward the hall. I had nowhere to go but to duck into the bathroom, where he'd likely see me anyway. As quietly as I could, I stepped into the tub and huddled behind the shower curtain.

The light in the front room snapped off, and Kyle's shoes thudded across the floor. His dark shape passed by the bathroom, then I heard the creak of the door as it opened. A slash of light streaked across the hallway before narrowing once again. I didn't breathe easy until the door slammed shut.

What had Kyle been looking for? Some kind of evidence of his assignation with Natasha? Had he killed her here and then dragged her body out to the cabana? Unlikely. There probably would have been drag marks in the sand, not to mention sand all over her. I was no expert, but it looked to me like she'd been killed right there on the beach.

I was tempted to do a search myself. Why not? Clearly, Natasha had been in the room the night she died or Kyle wouldn't have gone straight for it the minute he had a chance.

Stepping out from behind the shower curtain, I crept toward the hallway. I glanced left and right before snapping on the light in the hall. I wasn't sure where to start, but since Kyle had been searching the couch, that seemed a logical place. Maybe in his haste, he'd overlooked something.

I'd just lifted the first couch cushion when the scrape of something against the tile behind me sent chills up my spine. I froze before turning around very slowly.

"Well, now," Kyle said, his face an angry mask. "What have we here? A nosey little mouse come to poke into what isn't her business. What shall we do about that little mouse?"

I opened my mouth, but nothing came out except a squeak. For in Kyle's hand was clutched a very sharp knife.

Chapter 7
A Clue

"Now, Kyle," I said, holding up my hands in the universal sign of surrender. "Let's not be hasty." I backed up until my legs hit the mattress of the nearest bed. Kyle was going to kill me. *I really should listen to Cheryl more often.*

"I'm not going to hurt you," he said with a frustrated snort.

"What?" He wasn't going to kill me? I felt a flood of relief followed by complete and utter confusion. "You're not going to kill me?" I blurted.

He gave me a baffled look. "Why would I do that?"

I stabbed a finger in his general direction. "You're brandishing a knife."

He stared down at the knife in his hand as if he'd forgotten it was there. "Oh, that," he said, staring at the knife in his hand as if he'd never seen it before. "I thought *you* were the killer after *me.*"

"Well, that's ridiculous. I'm the one who found the body. Why would I kill you?"

"You could have been a burglar or something." He frowned. "Well, you are, I guess, but I mean a dangerous one."

"Oh, yes," I said dryly. "I'm exceptionally dangerous. Now would you put that thing down and tell me why you lied to me?"

He sighed and padded back to the kitchen, where he tossed the knife into the sink. Then he turned to me, resignation written all over his face. "Come on. Would *you* admit you'd banged a murder victim, like, minutes before her death?"

"Er, no. Certainly not." I tried not to wince at the word "bang." Not to be a fuddy-duddy or anything, but it was just so...uncouth. There were a lot more interesting and creative words for such an...event. "So, why did you come back? To the room I mean?"

He shrugged, running a hand through his spiky hair. "To make sure nothing got left behind. In case the police search the room."

I would have bought it if I hadn't seen the search. He'd been looking for something specific. Of that, I had no doubt. "What did you leave behind?"

"I lost my key card, okay? I figured even if they couldn't trace it to me, it probably had my fingerprints on it or something. I thought maybe it got lost in the couch, but it isn't here, so I'm good." He seemed genuinely relieved.

"Won't your boss want to know where the card went?" I asked.

"Naw. Guests lose their cards all the time. Or take them home or magnetically wipe them. It's not uncommon to end up with missing cards. It was keyed in under the manager's name anyway. I ain't dumb enough to put it under my own name." He grinned cockily as if he'd done something super smart. Frankly I was surprised he'd been that forward thinking. From what I'd seen of him, he pretty much appeared to let his hormones do the thinking.

I eyeballed him thoughtfully. Kyle might be guilty of fornication with a woman old enough to be his mother (as well as having very poor taste in women), but he hadn't done anything an innocent person wouldn't have done. Heck, if I could have lied to the police about finding Natasha's body, I probably would have. I just hadn't thought they'd suspect me. Silly me.

I wasn't quite ready to write him off the suspect list entirely, but he wasn't looking nearly as suspicious as I'd originally thought. Everything could be easily explained. And what motive did he have anyway? I honestly couldn't think of one.

"Listen, you aren't going to tell anyone are you?" Kyle asked, looking suddenly worried. "I could lose my job, and I really need it."

"Don't worry," I assured him. "As far as I'm concerned, your boss doesn't need to know about any of this."

He breathed a sigh of relief. "Thanks." He flashed a genuine grin, not the fake one from the bar. "I owe you one."

"Sure kid." What I didn't say was that I planned to tell Detective Hottie first chance I got. Anything less would be illegal. Messing with an investigation or something, and I'd already done plenty of that. Besides, it might get Costa off Cheryl's and my back.

We said a brief goodbye at the door, and Kyle took off for parts unknown. I started for the elevator when a hiss from somewhere to my right startled me so bad I nearly swallowed my tongue. I whipped around only to find a dark, huddled shape in the shadows behind a giant potted palm. I was pretty sure I knew who it was.

"Cheryl, is that you?"

"Keep your voice down."

"No need. Kyle already caught me."

She stood up, sunlight picking out the reds and golds in her mostly brown hair. She was wearing a navy blue t-shirt with the phrase "Obstinate, headstrong girl" in white, swirly letters.

"What?" She sounded horrified.

I waved off her concern. "Don't worry. We talked it out. He had a perfectly reasonable explanation." I quickly told her about my conversation with Kyle.

"So, he's not a suspect then?" she asked doubtfully.

"I wouldn't say that exactly, but he's low on the list. His explanation made sense. Besides, what motive would he have? He barely knew Natasha, and she was much older than he. I have no doubt she was a fling. Probably one of many. Kyle's a good-looking kid, for his age, and gets plenty of attention from guests. He doesn't exactly strike me as being above taking advantage of said attention. Natasha was just another notch in the bedpost, so to speak."

"Good point," Cheryl said. She propped her hands on her hips. "So now what?"

I checked the time on my phone. "It's too late to call Costa, so I'll ring him in the morning. How about we grab a nightcap and see if anything interesting is happening?"

She grinned. "Sounds like a plan."

# # #

It was early enough that the Flying Fish was still open. NWA Conference attendees, clearly marked by the blue badges hanging from lanyards around their necks, huddled in groups around long tables, chatting in hushed tones. It was clear that Natasha's murder was the topic on everyone's minds. Couldn't say I blamed them. She seemed to be taking up more than her fair share of space in my head.

On the far side of the room, I caught sight of two women sitting alone. Both were what one might consider "of a certain age." They were clearly caught in an intense argument. I nudged Cheryl. "Look at that."

She squinted. "Is that Yvonne Kittering? Natasha's editor from Romantic Press?" she asked, subtly indicating the woman on the right. She had the vague outline of a fireplug, square and squat, with muddy brown eyes and short, graying hair. An unlit cigarette was clutched between two fingers and a bottle of antacids sat beside her wine glass.

I nodded. "It is. And it looks like she's having a heated conversation with Natasha's personal assistant."

Cheryl frowned. "That doesn't look like Piper."

"No, it's the new one. Greta something."

"Oh, yeah. Morris."

It was well known in the romance community that Natasha had fired her original PA, Piper Ross, the woman who'd been with her since the beginning, before she'd gotten successful. Word on the circuit was that Piper and Jason Winters had gotten extremely cozy, and Natasha found out. She'd fired the former and began divorce proceedings on the latter. Although I'd never heard that Piper cared much about getting fired. Natasha had been a major pain to work for even back then, although perhaps not as big a diva as she eventually became.

In any case, Natasha's new PA, Greta Morris, was about as different from her old PA as two women could be. While Piper was young, attractive, and a go-getter, Greta was past middle age, plump, graying, and scared of her own shadow.

I pulled Cheryl to an empty table not far from the two women. "Let's see if we can learn anything."

"You mean eavesdrop?" she hissed.

I shrugged. "If you insist." It was semantics, really. If I was going to learn anything at all, underhanded tactics would be involved. It wasn't like I could march up to either woman and ask them if they bumped off Natasha.

We sat down as quietly as possible, trying to look natural and inconspicuous. I'm not sure we were terribly successful, but Yvonne and Greta were so deep in conversation they didn't even look up when the waiter came to take our order.

Unfortunately the Flying Fish didn't serve blackberry bourbon. I needed a clear head, anyway, so I ordered iced tea. Cheryl asked for a beer.

"What?" she hissed when I shot her a look. "I need to calm my nerves. I swear you're going to give me heart palpations with all this investigating nonsense."

I hushed her. The last thing we needed was people cottoning on to our investigation. Subtlety was key here.

The women's voices grew louder by the minute. By the time the waiter brought our order, they were practically screaming. I expected that from Yvonne—she and Natasha had more than one screaming match over the years—but from Greta it was totally unexpected.

"It wasn't my idea," Greta all but shouted. "You're the one who got me into this. I won't go down for—."

"Shut up, you fool," Yvonne snapped. "Do you want everyone to know about..." she trailed off. Her small, muddy brown eyes darted around the Flying Fish while everyone else pretended to be engrossed in their drinks. "Come on. We'll continue this conversation elsewhere." She stood up and tossed a few bills on the table before storming out, Greta followed along in her wake. Both of the women were flushed, eyes snapping with anger.

I leaned closer to Cheryl. "Come on, let's follow them."

Before either of us could budge from our seats, a new player arrived. "Hello, ladies. Is this seat taken?"

Cheryl beamed up at Lucas Salvatore. "Of course not. Please sit down."

I all but growled in frustration. Yvonne and Greta had disappeared from sight. I had no idea what direction they'd gone, and now I'd never know what they were arguing about. What if it was something important?

"I hope I'm not interrupting something," Lucas said smoothly, taking a seat across from me. It was obvious from his expression he knew very well he'd interrupted.

I found myself suddenly ensnared in his gray eyes and barely refrained from shaking my head. What was wrong with me? I did not have time to moon over some writer dude. I had a mystery to solve.

I opened my mouth to tell him that he was, indeed, interrupting something when Cheryl barged in. "Oh, no, not at all, Lucas. It's so good to see you again." Good grief, the girl could gush.

After placing his drink order with the waiter, he leaned back, fingers laced behind his head. "So how goes the investigation?"

I glared at him. "Why don't you announce it to the entire bar?"

He laughed. "I wouldn't worry. Everyone else is more interested in speculating about Yvonne and Greta's argument."

"You heard that?" Cheryl asked.

"Naturally."

I leaned forward eagerly. "Do you know what it was about?"

A slow grin spread across his handsome face. "Perhaps. What is it worth to you?"

My eyes narrowed. "Stop messing around and tell me, or else..." I had no idea what to threaten him with, but hopefully he'd get the message.

He held out his hands in supplication. "Mercy." I swear he was laughing at me. "Now, keep in mind, this is all second- and third-hand information, but what I heard is that Natasha was being courted by a new acquisitions editor at a competing publishing house."

My eyes widened. "Natasha is leaving Romantic Press?"

"I don't know for sure," Lucas admitted, "but that's the rumor. Yvonne had some kind of deal going with Greta, and apparently Greta failed to deliver."

Cheryl leaned forward, buzzing with excitement. She did love a good piece of gossip. I could relate. "What kind of deal? Like spying on Natasha or something?"

"I honestly don't know, but that would make sense, wouldn't it?"

Now it was me buzzing with excitement. What if Greta had been spying on Natasha for Yvonne, and Natasha had found out? Confronted Greta. If she fired Piper over sleeping with Jason, she'd for sure fire Greta over spying, and from what I understood, Natasha was Greta's only client. Natasha could easily make sure Greta never got hired again. It would totally give Greta a motive for murdering Natasha.

Or maybe it was Yvonne. Maybe she got so angry with Natasha about leaving her and Romantic Press that she confronted Natasha on the beach. They argued and *blamo!* Natasha ends up dead. Yes, I could definitely see it going either way.

"Forget about Yvonne and Greta for a minute," Cheryl said, interrupting my thoughts. "What about the bracelet?"

"Bracelet?" Lucas perked up.

I explained where and how I found the bracelet and my plan for it. Then I told them both about how I'd shown it to Kyle. "I'm certain he recognized it, but he's a cagey one. He pretended not to recognize it."

"Why would he do that?" Cheryl asked.

I shrugged. "Who knows?"

"Can I see it?" Lucas asked.

I pulled the silver bracelet from my handbag and gave it to him. "There's an etching on the back, but it's hard to see."

He held it up to the light, frowning slightly as he inspected the inside of the jewelry. "Yes, I see it. It's well worn, but I am fairly certain the first letter is an 'A.' The second is almost impossible to make out. 'C' maybe? I can't really tell."

He handed the bracelet back. It was my turn to hold it up to the light and squint at it. He was right. It was impossible to make out the second letter. Not that the initials would help much. There must be a hundred women at the Fairwinds Resort whose names began with the letter "A."

Still, it was interesting. I needed to find out if Kyle knew a woman with an "A" name. I was still certain he'd recognized it. I'd half expected it to be Natasha's, but there was no way she'd have worn something with another woman's initials. She just didn't roll that way.

Lucas leaned forward. "Penny for your thoughts."

I smiled smugly. "Oh, believe me, they're worth a whole lot more than that."

He raised one black eyebrow. "A dollar?"

I snorted with amusement as I waved the waiter over to pay. I started to pull out my keycard to charge my room when Lucas waved me off. "My treat."

"Thank you."

He nodded graciously.

I smirked. "But I'm still not telling you."

Chapter 8
The Mysterious Newcomer

The next morning I put in a call for Detective Costa. Reluctantly, mind you. Costa's suspiciousness freaked me out, and I'd yet to find any proof to clear my and Cheryl's names. But I'd seen crime shows on TV. I knew what happened when you withheld important information from the police, and I did not want to end up on the six o'clock news wearing handcuffs. I'd be getting a call from my mother for sure.

The desk sergeant put me through to Costa's cell phone, which surprised me. I wasn't sure that was a good thing. More like "this chick is a suspect and I'm waiting for her to confess" sort of thing.

"Go for Costa." His voice boomed through the tiny speaker.

Rather brusque way to answer the phone, don't you think? "Uh, this is Viola Roberts."

The pause was a little lengthier than I would have liked. "How can I help you, Ms. Roberts?"

Oh, so smooth. I cleared my throat. "I have some information you might find interesting."

Another brief pause. "I'm on my way."

"Wait—" But he'd already hung up. Doggonnit. Where was I supposed to meet him? Was he coming to my room? I stared down at myself. I was still in pajamas, no makeup, and my hair was a mess. I hadn't had a shower either. I sniffed my armpit. Ew.

71

It wasn't unusual for me to skip a day of showering when on a deadline, but this was not such a time. Exposing the world, or even Costa, to my unwashed self was not on the agenda.

There wasn't time for a proper shower, so I did a spit-bath thing, swiped on some deodorant, and ran a comb through my hair before smushing in some pomade. Not much an improvement, but there was no help for it. I was debating my outfit for the day when someone banged on the door. My stomach heaved with dread. Sure enough, standing on the other side of the peephole was Detective Hottie, and he looked good enough to eat. Naturally, I looked like I'd been caught in a tornado.

"Give me a second," I called through the closed door.

"Make it snappy."

I rolled my eyes, but did as he ordered. I whipped off my pajamas and threw on a pair of navy blue capris and a hot-pink t-shirt.

With a sigh, I threw open the door and forced a cheery smile. "Detective. How nice to see you. Come in."

He was wearing the same rumpled suit he'd worn the first time I met him. At least I assumed it was the same one. It looked the same. He followed me past the messy bedroom and into the living area. "Would you like some coffee?" *Cops drink coffee, right? That isn't just a movie thing?*

"Thank you. No."

"Well, I need some," I said, busying myself with preparing my morning beverage. Actually, what I needed was some hard liquor, but it was way too early for that. "Have a seat." I waved to the couch.

"Thanks, but I'll stand."

"Suit yourself. How can I help you?"

"You called me, remember?"

Oh, right. "Of course." I grabbed the French vanilla creamer from the fridge and poured a generous dollop into a mug. "I overheard a conversation last night I thought you'd find of interest."

One black eyebrow went up, but he remained silent. Great. He wasn't going to make this easy on me.

"I was at the Flying Fish Grill with some friends last night, and I saw two of your suspects arguing with each other."

"How do you know they're my suspects?" he asked, giving me a bland look.

I barely refrained from giving me an eye roll. "Because if they're not, you're not very good at your job." It came out a little more snarky than I intended.

His lips quirked. Hopefully in amusement. I could use some goodwill right about now. "Go on."

"I assume you've questioned Natasha's editor, Yvonne Kitterage? And her current personal assistant, Greta?"

He didn't give any indication he'd done so. Just stared at me with gimlet eyes. Man, he was disconcerting.

"Well," I tried not to squirm, instead splashing dark liquid into my mug. I took a long swallow. Nirvana. "They were at the Flying Fish, and they were arguing about something."

"What were they arguing about?"

"Er, well, it wasn't very clear. First Greta said, 'It wasn't my idea.' And then she said something about Yvonne being the one who got her into 'this' —whatever 'this' was—and that she wasn't going down for it. Then Yvonne got really mad and told her to shut up and did Greta want everyone to know about...whatever it was they were up to. Then they went elsewhere to finish the conversation. I was going to follow them to find out what it was all about, but, well, I got waylaid."

Detective Costa's eyes narrowed. "And you thought this was important enough to have me come all the way out here?"

I gritted my teeth hard enough to make my jaw hurt. "Well, don't you? Two major suspects arguing right after the murder? I mean it's obvious it had something to do with all this."

"Is it?" He seemed unimpressed.

I was irritated. Was he purposely being dense? I decided to spell it out for him. "Look, what if Yvonne and Greta were in on it? The murder, I mean. They both had motive. What if they decided to off Natasha, and that's what they were talking about?"

"That's a lot of supposition, Ms. Roberts. I don't deal in guesswork. I deal in facts."

I hated when he called me "Ms. Roberts." It sounded so stuffy. I ground my teeth, barely resisting the urge to call him an idiot. "But they *are* suspects, aren't they? And you've got to admit that them having an argument like that is suspicious."

He leaned forward, his blue eyes icy. "No. I don't have to admit any such thing. Listen to me very carefully, Ms. Roberts. I'm only going to say this once. Stay out of my investigation."

"Or what?" I heard myself blurt.

"Or I will lock you up and throw away the key."

# # #

"Wow. What a jerk," Cheryl said indignantly over breakfast later that morning. "How dare he threaten you!"

I knew I could count on Cheryl to be on my side. "I know. But I did what I could, and he can't accuse me of withholding information. Unless you count the bracelet, but he doesn't know about that." All I needed was a rap sheet. Although maybe a little scandal would be good for sales. You never knew.

She nodded, stabbing her fork into a syrup drenched waffle. "So, you're going to stop investigating now, right?"

"No way," I said, digging into my own Eggs Benedict. "Not until I clear our names."

She groaned and opened her mouth, surely to tell me all the horrible reasons my investigation was a bad idea, when we were interrupted once again by Lucas Salvatore. He looked particularly delicious in worn jeans and a snug, black t-shirt.

"Good morning, ladies."

I mumbled a greeting. Cheryl was much friendlier.

He sank into the chair next to me without asking. "Are you ladies planning to attend the tour?"

I gave him a blank stare.

"What tour?" Cheryl piped up around a mouthful of waffle.

"The tour of the haunted mansion, of course." He grinned, showing off his perfect pearly whites. He really did have a nice smile. Darn him.

I started to ask what haunted mansion he was talking about when Cheryl spoke up. "Oh, you mean the pink hotel down the road?" At his nod, she turned to me. "Remember? The cab driver said it was the second most haunted building in all of Florida. Oh, we have to go. Don't you think it would be fun?"

I, for one, did not believe in ghosts. Mostly I considered what people thought of as spirits from the Great Beyond to be nothing more than a result of overactive imaginations. But Cheryl was so excited, and Lucas was grinning in that sexy way of his. How could I say no? Besides, historical buildings were always of interest to me. You never knew when they would fit into a story, though I doubted a Florida hotel would work in a bodice-ripping Western. Still, I agreed to join the tour which pretty much made Cheryl's day. Lucas looked happy about it, too, though I was betting it was more for Cheryl's sake than mine. Sure he'd been very personable over drinks that first night, but Cheryl seemed more his type. They had a lot in common. Both thriller writers. Both athletic and good looking. Not that I'm not an attractive woman, but generally men gravitate toward

Cheryl. Believe me, I'm fine with it. I like being single. Nobody to steal the remote from me or leave the toilet seat up.

Maybe in addition to solving Natasha's murder, I could play matchmaker. Now there was a thought. I bet I'd be good at it, too. Not to sound smug, but I write romance for a living, after all.

The tour group had rented a van for the trip, and we climbed aboard—some of us less gracefully than others. There was just no graceful way to squeeze oneself between a van wall and a bench seat, especially when one had an ample backside. By the time I was in my seat, the combination of the afternoon heat, humidity, and exertion had wilted my hair, melted my makeup, and turned my face the color of a cherry tomato.

Cheryl looked cool as a cucumber. Well, maybe there was a little bit of a "glow" about her, but she still looked great even sweaty. Lucas looked fantastic, as though the heat didn't even bother him. The big jerk.

I sighed. It wasn't fair.

Also on the mini bus were a couple of older ladies, perhaps in their sixties. Both were on the plump side with white hair and flowy, bright-colored clothing. One had red-framed cat's eye glasses. They looked vaguely familiar. I introduced myself and Cheryl.

The one with the glasses leaned across the seat and shook my hand vigorously. "Nice to meet you, Viola. Cheryl," she boomed. "Maggie Vane. Mysteries. Cozy." She clipped each word like it was its own sentence. "This here is Louisa Lee Lambert. Contemporary romances. Just call her Lu."

Lu beamed at me, but didn't say a word. I noticed she was wearing hot-pink, heart-shaped earrings that dangled from her earlobes. Every time she turned her head, they sparkled in the sunlight. Apparently Lu was fond of glitter.

Maggie slapped Lucas on the back. "And who are you, handsome?"

I swear Lucas blushed as he shook Maggie's hand. "Lucas. Thrillers."

Maggie raised one white eyebrow, a knowing look crossing her creased face. "Are you that Salvatore fellow everyone is going on about?"

"One and the same," he admitted. Yep. Definitely blushing.

"Splendid." She sat back with satisfaction. "We should compare notes later. Cozy versus thriller. Writing. Marketing. Those kind of shenanigans." She punctuated her words with gusto in a broad, slightly nasally East Coast accent.

"I would enjoy that," he said graciously.

I noted that, other than the driver, Lucas was the only man in the vehicle. Apparently haunted mansions didn't appeal to as many gentleman writers as one might have thought. Interesting since ghost-hunting shows tended to lean heavily to the male arena. "All at the bar," Maggie barked.

"Huh?" I glanced at her, confused by her non-sequitur.

"The men. All at the bar. Why they come to these things mostly. Conferences, I mean."

"Ah. I see." I didn't really, but then I'd been single for a long time, and my previous relationships had proven I understood little about the opposite gender. Or rather, I understood too much, which was probably worse.

Just as the driver started the engine, a figure dashed toward the van, waving a floppy white sunhat. A large green and white striped bag banged wildly against her side as her silver flip-flops slapped against the hot asphalt.

"Oh my word," Cheryl whispered, leaning forward to squint through the window. "That's Piper."

I peered around her shoulder. Sure enough, the red hair was unmistakable. The woman running toward us was none other than Piper Ross, Natasha's former assistant. The woman at least partially responsible for the breakup of Natasha's marriage, although I held Jason equally responsible since he couldn't keep it in his pants. It took two to tango and all that.

I smiled widely, excited about the prospect of more sleuthing. "Oh, this is going to be an interesting adventure."

I ignored Cheryl's groan.

Chapter 9
A Suspicious Event

Piper Ross paused in front of the open van door, holding her floppy hat up to shade her eyes. I noticed there was a giant red poppy glued to one side. Very colorful. "Is this the van to the haunted place?" She blinked big, pretty, green eyes rimmed with thick, dark lashes. They looked fake, but I had a feeling they were real. Darn her.

The driver beamed down at her, his basset-hound face getting an instant facelift. "Sure, miss. Hop in."

She gave him a charming smile, revealing a dimple in her left cheek, and climbed aboard without so much as a single drop of sweat marring her perfect face. Her eyes lit up when she saw Lucas, and she immediately squeezed in next to him. I held back a growl. It was silly of me to get jealous, but really it was for Cheryl's sake. Although Cheryl seemed not to notice.

It wasn't that I had a personal thing against Piper. It was just that she was so darn...flawless. At five foot eight and a hundred thirty pounds tops, she had the perfect figure. At least according to today's standards. Me, I'd have been in vogue about fifty years or so ago.

With her milky-white skin, flaming-red hair, and slightly tilted green eyes, she was, in a word, perfect. No wonder Jason had tossed Natasha for her. I probably would have, too. Especially if her personality was anything like her looks. I couldn't imagine Natasha had been an easy person to live with. Still, it didn't justify what they'd done, to my way of thinking.

Piper buckled herself in and gave the driver another blinding smile. "Ready when you are." Even her voice was charming and sexy, doggone it.

As the van swung out into traffic, Maggie and Lu began talking excitedly about the history of the mansion we were to visit. Well, Maggie started chatting. Lu mostly nodded her head, earrings shooting colorful sparks of light around the van.

I expected Piper to start chatting Lucas up, but instead she bent over her smart phone, stabbing rapidly at the screen with her forefinger. I tried to see what she was typing, but all I could see was that it was a text…and it was to Jason Winters. Big surprise. The two were still a couple, after all. Which was so odd. I mean Jason was not bad looking, but he was at least twenty years older than Piper, pudgy around the middle, and balding. Not to mention that since the split with Natasha, he was out of a job. Not the sort of person I expected a woman like Piper to go for. At least not in the long run. Although now Jason would probably inherit Natasha's money and that meant he'd be a very rich man.

Unless, of course, Natasha had changed her will or something. Which was possible. Even likely. I made a mental note to find out who inherited. Whoever it was would have an excellent motive. But if it wasn't Jason, why would Piper still be with him? Could they actually be in love? I'd need to watch them more closely to decide. Anything was possible. Love was crazy like that.

Time to dive in. I cleared my throat. "You're Piper Ross, right?"

She glanced up from the screen, startled. A tiny frown line marred her forehead before smoothing away. "Um, yes. Why?"

I gave her a bland smile. "Viola Roberts. I'm really sorry about Natasha. I know you worked for her for a long time."

A scowl crossed her face, quickly replaced by that dazzling smile. Aha! So, Piper Ross wasn't so perfect and perky. Whatever she might pretend in public, she really didn't like Natasha.

"Oh, yes. It's very sad, isn't it?" she said, not sounding at all sincere.

"Very. Such a shocking thing, you know."

"Oh, yes." She didn't sound at all shocked.

"Jason isn't interested in haunted mansions, I take it?"

She looked confused for a moment. "Oh, he has a meeting today. With some lawyer." She shrugged. "I don't really understand legal stuff, and I figured it would be boring just sitting around the hotel."

So, Piper was playing the ditzy young thing. I didn't buy it for a moment. The woman who helped Natasha claw her way to the top was not a stupid woman, but I figured it would behoove me to play along.

"Oh, I hear you." A lawyer. How interesting. Could it be an estate lawyer? Or perhaps a criminal one?

"Do you know which lawyer Jason is seeing?" I blurted.

Her eyes narrowed suspiciously. "Why?"

"Well," I scrambled for a reason other than the obvious, "research, you know. For my next book."

"Don't you write historicals?" she asked.

"Sure. Mostly. But I'm expanding into mysteries, and there's a lawyer in my novel, you see. Only I don't know any lawyers. I'd love to ask questions."

She seemed to relax somewhat, the dopey expression settling over her like the perfect mask it was. She gave a little shrug. "Sorry. No idea. You'll have to ask Jason." She turned back to her phone screen.

I found it odd that Jason wouldn't tell her what lawyer he was meeting or that she would care so little about it, but I didn't want to press my luck. Lucas eyed me over the top of Piper's head. From his expression, he knew exactly what I was up to. Well, more power to him.

I searched for something else to ask her. Not that I was lacking in questions, but it was all about the phrasing. Piper wasn't just a pretty face, obviously. She was on high alert, and I didn't want her to realize I was more than just another nosey writer.

Cheryl came to my rescue. "Gosh, that was awful, wasn't it? Did you know Viola found the body? I mean, I didn't know anything about it until I woke up the next morning." She shuddered as she turned to me with wide eyes. "You're just so brave."

I almost snorted with laughter at her innocent act. "Didn't have much choice, did I? Although I'll think twice before walking the beach at night again, let me tell you. What if the killer was lurking in the dark?"

"You could have been killed!" Maggie boomed from the front. I hadn't realized that she and Lu were listening.

Cheryl nodded, expression eager. "That's what I keep saying. I'm so glad I went straight to bed. Where were you when you heard about it, Maggie?"

Light glinted off the lenses of Maggie's glasses. "Lu and I were at breakfast. Annabelle MacDonald told us over coffee. You know Annabelle, right? She writes those Highland romances. Popular what with that show on TV now."

I nodded. I didn't know Annabelle personally, but I was familiar with her work. They mostly featured pictures of half-naked men in kilts on the covers. I approved most heartily.

"How about you, Piper?" Cheryl asked innocently. "How did you hear? You must have been really shocked since you used to work with her and everything."

"Oh, of course. Very shocked," Piper agreed pleasantly. "Of course, we didn't know anything about it until the police came to Jason's room to notify him."

And question him, no doubt. He was, after all, next of kin. Plus, didn't they always suspect the spouse first?

"We went to bed right after the party," Piper continued. "Jason was kind of drunk."

I wondered if she was telling the truth. And if Jason was so drunk, though from what I'd seen he hadn't been but perhaps a little tipsy, could Piper have slipped out without him knowing and murdered Natasha? Anything was possible. And Piper had so many motives: revenge for Natasha firing her, getting her hand on Natasha's money (if Jason was the heir), just plain old hatred. Time would tell, but I was keeping a close eye on the nearly perfect Piper.

I slanted a glance toward Lucas, who was looking particularly handsome in a heather gray t-shirt that matched his eyes. He'd changed since breakfast. I'd be keeping an eye on the Handsome Author Dude, too. Not because I suspected him of murder, but because I didn't want him falling for Piper's obvious charms. For Cheryl's sake, of course.

# # #

As we spilled out of the van, we were greeted by a gray-haired gentleman dressed neatly in khaki slacks and a white button-down shirt. His nametag proclaimed him to be "George," and he had the most enormous moustache I'd ever seen on anyone born after 1800.

"Hiya folks." He waved us over. "Ready to see some ghosts?" He beamed at us.

I had a hard time believing we'd see anything in broad daylight—weren't ghosts supposed to be most active at night?—but George was very enthusiastic, as were Maggie and Lu. Even Cheryl seemed excited, and Lucas already had a notebook and pen out. Very old school. Piper, oddly enough, seemed bored by the whole thing, examining her cuticles and sighing heavily like she was being put upon. Which led a person to wonder why she'd bothered to come? Surely there was plenty to do back at the resort if ghost hunting wasn't her thing.

With the van empty, the driver promised to collect us in ninety minutes, then zipped out of the parking lot. The hot sun glared down, melting any remaining makeup from my face. No doubt I looked like a raccoon. A frizzy-haired raccoon. The humidity was turning my hair into something out of a bad '50s sci-fi movie. One where the heroine got electrocuted.

George led us up the wide front steps and through the double doors into the hotel lobby. He was already cheerfully informing us of the details of the original owner's death and how he was said to haunt the place. I tried really hard not to roll my eyes. I wouldn't say I was a skeptic exactly. More that I preferred to see the evidence of something, and I'd yet to see any evidence that ghosts were real.

Everyone else seemed eager to catch all the gory details. Only Piper was as unimpressed as I was, surreptitiously sneaking glances at her phone. She wasn't texting, so I wondered if she was waiting for a call, and if so, from whom? Maybe she was planning to meet someone at the Don CeSar.

A little bubble of excitement zinged at the thought. How clandestine! Maybe it was a secret lover. Maybe she was cheating on Jason. Scandal!

Inside, the hotel was like something out of a fairy tale. The wide entry hall was paved in ivory marble and lined on either side with matching marble pillars.

Overhead, massive gold and crystal chandeliers bathed the place in sparkling light. Everything was bright, elegant, and exactly the opposite of what I expected from a haunted mansion.

George had switched to stories of a ghost in a white suit walking along the beach. Apparently also the original owner. I supposed there were worse ways to spend the afterlife.

As he led us upstairs, George launched into an account of a female ghost in a flowing gown often spotted walking the hotel halls. "A raven-haired beauty, she is."

"Have you actually seen her?" Cheryl asked breathlessly. Her eyes were wide, and she had her cell phone out, videoing the tour.

"You bet," George said with a grin. "It was late one night. I'd just finished a tour and was rounding this very corner." With a dramatic flourish, he waved to the corner in question, which, frankly, looked like every other corner in the hotel. "And there she was. Staring out the window as if waiting for her true love," he finished melodramatically.

Lu sighed at the romantic tale. Maggie strode to the corner to look out the window as if expecting the lady ghost to appear immediately.

As George droned on about other ghost sightings, I wandered a bit away from the others toward the sweeping staircase. Honestly, I was more interested in the architecture and design of the place. According to George, it had been built in the 1920s. Very *Great Gatsby*.

A little late for my era, but perhaps I could write a story about it. Some Western cowboy, maybe from Montana, goes east for...something. Hmm... An inheritance, maybe? He would meet a rich heiress, and then...

Before I could finish my thought, I felt a hard shove from behind. I stumbled, my foot hitting the top step. Somebody screamed. And then I was falling.

Chapter 10
Appointment with Death

For a brief moment, I thought about how people talk about their hearts jumping into their throats. Because I was pretty sure mine actually did.

It was as if time ceased to exist. Everything around me froze as I tumbled in slow motion through empty air. And then it sped up as I crashed, knees first, into the first step. Flailing like a lunatic, I managed to grab the balustrade and halt myself mid-fall. I wrenched my shoulder in the process, but it was better than smashing my skull on the marble steps.

Above me, I could hear people shouting, but I wasn't sure what they were saying. My hearing was fuzzy all of a sudden.

Gasping for breath, I turned my head to glance up the staircase. The entire group was gathered at the top of the landing, horrified expressions plastered on their faces. Even Piper had been jarred from her ennui and appeared suitably startled.

"Oh, my goodness," Cheryl managed to gasp, her face so white it was if she'd seen a ghost. Mine. "What happened?" She clattered down the stairs, flip-flops slapping against the stone. "We heard you scream. Did you slip? You could have been killed." She tried to haul me to my feet, but only managed to wrench my already throbbing arm. I must have winced because she blanched even whiter. "You're hurt! Somebody call 911."

"Don't be ridiculous," I finally managed.

"I don't think that's necessary," Lucas interrupted, joining us. The stair was getting crowded. "Looks like she's in one piece. Just a few bumps and bruises?"

I nodded. "I'm fine. My shoulder hurts a bit, that's all. From where I grabbed the railing." And my knees throbbed like nobody's business. I was going to have some nice purple bruises in no time.

"What happened?" Cheryl repeated. "Did you slip?"

"No," I said, eyeing the watchers above. Having no idea who was the guilty party, or even if they were part of our group, I lowered my voice. "I was pushed."

For a minute, I was afraid Cheryl would pass out. "Somebody tried to kill you," she squeaked.

"Shh. Keep it down." I eyed the group again, but no one seemed to have heard her.

Lucas glanced up, too. "You think it was one of us?"

"Maybe, maybe not. But I don't want to let on I suspect anyone."

Lucas offered his arm and helped me limp up the stairs. After ensuring I was fine and receiving my refusal of a trip to the hospital, George continued the tour. I limped along behind the rest of the group with Cheryl all but glued to my side.

"You think this had anything to do with Natasha's murder?" she whispered.

"Of course it does," I said, trying to ignore the pain in my knees as I limped down yet another hall. "Being as that I don't usually get pushed down stairs, it has to be connected."

"But who would do that?"

I eyed her. "Other than the killer?"

Her eyes widened. "You think the killer is here? One of the group? Surely not."

I shrugged, holding back a wince as pain lanced through my shoulder. Maybe a trip to the doctor was in order after all. "Maybe. It's possible. I still haven't ruled out Piper. And then there's Lucas..."

"Oh, please." She rolled her eyes. "You know very well that Lucas didn't murder Natasha. And he would never push you down the stairs. Don't be silly."

I wasn't so sure, but I let it go for the moment. "There are other options."

"Lu and Maggie?" She actually giggled. "Those two lovelies? I don't think so. Can you really see either of them as a knife-wielding maniac?"

I had to admit I couldn't, but stranger things have happened. "There's another option."

"What?"

"The killer has a sidekick. Somebody helping them. Somebody who didn't commit the murder, but who is involved in the cover-up. Maybe that person is here."

"You're talking about Piper, aren't you?"

"Could be. Or could be any of the others." I mulled it over. "Or it could be someone outside the group. Someone lurking around. They could have followed us here. Seized an opportunity."

Cheryl glanced around as if the evil person was lurking in the planters or behind the velvet curtains. "Like who?"

"I don't know," I admitted. "It could be anybody. Likely someone from the Fairwinds, though. I mean, the killer has to be there. Who else would want to kill Natasha? And his, or her, sidekick is probably staying there, too."

"But what if the sidekick is staying somewhere else? You know, to throw us off the scent?"

Cheryl made a good point. And my suspect list just got a whole lot longer and a whole lot more complicated.

As the tour came to an end, George led us down the back stairs—not exactly comfortable going in my condition—and through the service hallways to the front lobby. All the while, he regaled us with tales of guests who'd had run-ins with ghosts at the hotel, all of whom had escaped their ordeals unscathed.

As we entered the lobby, I stopped short at the sight of a figure near the front desk. Dread filled me. I knew that figure.

"Drat," I hissed, eyeing the lobby for a place to hide.

"What is it?" Cheryl asked.

"Detective Hottie. Three o'clock."

Cheryl glanced toward the check-in desk and frowned. "What's Costa doing here?"

"Good question." I debated whether or not to storm up to him and demand answers. Was he stalking me? Did he have a lead?

Of course, there could have been a murder at the hotel, and he'd been called to investigate. It was his job, after all. Though I was certain we'd have noticed if there was a dead body lying around. Besides mine, I mean. Dodged that proverbial bullet.

But then he turned toward me, and all hope of new homicides was gone. Detective Costa was here for me.

He strode across the marble floor, long legs eating up the distance in no time. Too bad he considered me a suspect, because I'd be all over that in a hot minute. Okay, probably not. But I'd flirt a lot. As it was, I needed to play it cool. No sense riling him up. I was in hot enough water already, though I couldn't for the life of me figure out what I'd done this time.

"Well, well, Ms. Roberts. You do like to be right in the middle of trouble, don't you?" Detective Costa said, stopping in front of me. The entire tour group hovered around, ears perked. Great. An audience. Just what I needed.

"Detective Costa. Lovely to see you," I said in my best fake posh accent. "Whatever do you mean?"

His eyes narrowed. "Don't play the innocent, Ms. Roberts. This is serious business."

"Er, what is?" I was genuinely confused.

"I hear someone tried to push you down the stairs today."

"Oh, that." I waved my hand airily, bravely holding back a flinch as another stab of pain tore through my arm. Yep. I was going to need a doctor. "It was no big thing. I'm fine."

A muscle flexed in his jaw. "This time."

I eyed him, unsure what he meant. "What is that supposed to mean?"

He stepped right up in my personal space. I had to struggle against the impulse to take a step back. I wasn't about to let the man bully me.

"Ms. Roberts," he bit out.

"Viola," I said brightly.

"Viola," he all but growled, "someone tried to kill you today. And, just in case you didn't get the message through that thick skull of yours, that is serious business. You need to back off. Get your nose out of my investigation and back onto your little romance novels where they belong."

That got my hackles up. *Little* romance novels? How dare he belittle my career and my passion? I worked hard, gosh darnit, and I wasn't going to let some backwater detective dismiss who I was and what I, and my readers, loved.

I opened my mouth to blast him a good one, but Cheryl grabbed my arm and squeezed hard enough to make my eyes water. "Sure thing, Detective," she cooed, all but batting her lashes at him. "We'll get right on that." She dragged me away, still sputtering, before I could punch Detective Costa in his smug face.

"What was that all about?" I snarled.

She grinned. "It's called living to fight another day."

A slow smile replaced my scowl. "I like the way you think."

# # #

"You know who we need to talk to?" I said to Cheryl as we exited the van. The ride back to the Fairwinds had been uneventful. Everyone expressed the proper amount of shock and sympathy. No one seemed suspicious. Even Piper appeared genuinely concerned about my well-being.

Of course, she *could* be faking it, but was she that good of an actress? It was hard to say. She was certainly the only one there with a strong connection to a suspect. Other than Cheryl and me, of course, but that was just silliness. Piper Ross and Jason Winters were still together, which meant she could be in on it with Jason. If he was the killer.

"Let me guess. Jason Winters," Cheryl said dryly.

"He's probably got the best motive to murder Natasha."

"*If* he inherits," Cheryl reminded me. "Which may very well not be the case since they're in the middle of a divorce."

"True," I admitted. "Though it isn't finalized, and Natasha might not have changed her will. If she did, though, Jason would be the most likely person to know who does inherit."

"You could have asked Costa," Cheryl teased, eyes dancing.

I snorted. "I'd rather give myself a paper cut and pour lemon juice on it. That man is a menace."

"To you and your shenanigans maybe. He's just doing his job."

"Yeah, well, he should hurry up because I'm sick of us being suspects."

Cheryl shook her head. "Are you sure you don't need a doctor? You wrenched your shoulder pretty good."

I caught myself rubbing said shoulder. "I'm fine. A little ice and some ibuprofen and I'll be good as new tomorrow." Unlikely, but hope sprung eternal. What I did not want was to waste hours of my time in the ER.

"Look," she chirped, coming to a standstill in the middle of the lobby, much to the annoyance of a tiny woman in a giant red muumuu. "There's Jason. Looks like he's going into one of the sessions."

"That's odd," I said. "He's not a writer."

"But he took care of Natasha's marketing and whatnot for years. He knows his stuff," Cheryl reminded me. "Maybe with her gone, he's thinking of taking on other clients."

Especially now that Natasha wasn't around to badmouth him.

Cheryl had a point. But still, the whole thing was odd in my book. Jason being here at the conference, I mean. And bringing Piper with him. Without Natasha, neither of them had jobs in the industry. Natasha had blackballed them both. Another motive for murder. Piper and Jason were looking increasingly guilty in my book.

"Let's follow him," I said, taking off at a trot toward the rapidly closing conference room door.

"You can't question him in there," Cheryl hissed as we slipped inside.

"No," I agreed, "but we can watch him like hawks. If he's guilty, I'm not letting him get away with it."

Cheryl shook her head in exasperation, but followed me into the row immediately behind Jason. I tried to look interested in what the speaker had to say, but the long-winded lecture on marketing trends was so boring I could barely keep my eyes open. To keep myself occupied, and from staring at Jason the entire time, I pulled out my conference notebook and began jotting down thoughts. Reasons why Jason was guilty, naturally.

Reason 1: Natasha was divorcing him.

Granted, he'd been a big, fat cheater-pants, but some men had a hard time with semantics. Maybe Jason Winters was one of those...his bruised ego leading him to commit murder.

Reason 2: Because of the pending divorce, Jason had lost not only his wife, but his job and his lifestyle, too.

That was definitely reason for murder. People had killed for less. A lot less. Especially since I knew very well that Natasha made seven figures and Jason was now on unemployment.

Reason 3: Natasha had blackballed both Jason and Piper, which meant neither of them could get a job in the industry. And while Jason had a "real" job once upon a time, Piper had only ever worked with Natasha. She had zero experience with anything else. Not exactly hiring material.

Yep. Big time motive right there.

Reason 4: Jason might inherit a fortune. Or better yet, the rights to Natasha's books, which would net him a future fortune many times over.

That one was iffy, of course. It all rested on Jason being the one to actually inherit. Something I still needed to check on.

Reason 5: Natasha was a witch with a capital B.

Granted, that gave, like, seven billion people motive to murder her, but I liked to be thorough.

Oh, and Reason 6: Jason and Natasha had a massive argument right before Natasha was killed. Granted, it probably wasn't their first argument, but it had definitely been their last. That had to mean something. And while Piper wasn't there for the argument, that didn't necessarily clear her. She could have been an accomplice either before or after the fact.

The marketing lecture was winding down, and people were already gathering their things. Jason got up and slipped out while the speaker was still summing up his points.

"Come on." I grabbed Cheryl's arm. "We've got to follow him."

Cheryl rolled her eyes, but she came along. That was a best friend for you. She might think you were on the road to crazy, but she would go straight there with you.

Chapter 11
A Motive for Murder

We followed Jason out of the lecture hall and into the main lobby, now swamped with the early dinner crowd. Still, we had no trouble spotting Jason's stocky figure wending his way through the crowd, since most of the crowd was white haired and moving at a more relaxed pace than our quarry. The Fairwinds Resort was popular with retirees apparently. Wouldn't have been my first choice, but each to his or her own, I supposed.

As Jason passed a group of NWA attendees, he was stopped to talk with one of the men. While they chatted, Cheryl and I busied ourselves outside one of the meeting room doors, pretending we were waiting for the lecture inside to let out. A familiar-looking blond woman passed by my line of sight. It struck a chord, and I paused for a moment. It couldn't be.

"Keep your eye on Jason," I hissed.

"Why?" Cheryl hissed back. "What are you—"

But I didn't let her finish. Instead I took off after the blond woman. She wasn't moving very fast, so I caught up with her quickly.

"Natasha?" It was insane of course. I knew she was dead. I'd found the body myself, but the woman in front of me looked so much like the dead diva, my heart literally pounded wildly in my chest.

The blonde didn't turn around. "Natasha?" I tapped her on the shoulder, and she spun to face me.

It wasn't Natasha. This woman was in her early twenties, her face unmarred by plastic surgery. Pretty, but unremarkable. Other than being the right shape and coloring, she looked nothing like Natasha. She was also wearing a smock with the logo of the resort spa stitched over her left breast. She was clearly a resort employee.

"May I help you?" She gave me a bland smile.

"Uh, no. Sorry. Thought you were someone else."

She gave a shrug. "It happens. Have a nice evening." And with that she twirled around gracefully and continued on her merry way. With a sigh, I made my way back to Cheryl, quickly catching her up on the not-Natasha sighting.

Jason finished his conversation and continued across the lobby. His pace picked up once he exited the main building and hit the courtyard. We hurried to match his speed without being too obvious.

"Where do you suppose he's going?" Cheryl asked. She wasn't the least bit out of breath. In fact, she looked cool as the proverbial cucumber despite the heat and humidity. Meanwhile, I was panting and sticky, the armpits of my shirt suspiciously soggy. There wasn't enough deodorant in the world to get me through this week without having to wash some shirts in the sink of my room.

I shrugged. "His room maybe?" It was in the direction we were going. "Or to meet up with his co-conspirator."

Cheryl's eyes widened. "Piper?"

"Who else? I bet dollars to donuts they're in on this together."

"We still don't know for sure Jason inherits. Maybe he doesn't."

"They'd still have motive. Revenge if nothing else."

Cheryl sighed. "True. Just...Piper seemed so nice. I have a hard time imagining her in on it."

"That's because you're a nice person instead of a suspicious so-and-so like me."

She held back a giggle. "You're a nice person, too."

I snorted. "Have you met me?"

She shook her head. "Really, Viola, you do say the oddest things sometimes."

Which was probably why we were friends. Not the *me saying odd things* part, but the *her believing I was a nice person* part. I supposed I was nice, as much as anybody, but while Cheryl always believed the best in people, I usually suspected them of being serial killers. It came from being weaned on murder mysteries.

"Look." Chery's whispered voice jarred me out of my woolgathering. "It's Piper's room."

Sure enough, Jason rapped on the room to Piper's door. It swung open almost immediately, so she'd obviously been expecting him. Maybe she'd been waiting to report her failed attempt to murder me?

Piper wrapped her arms around Jason's neck and dragged him inside, all the while peppering him with kisses. It was like a really bad romance movie. Or one of

Natasha's books. I might get sappy on occasion, but Natasha Winters had taken schmaltz to a whole new level.

"Well, darn." Cheryl sounded disappointed. "They're just being normal lovebirds."

"Were you hoping for another murder?" I asked dryly. "Mr. Winters in the hotel room with the ballpoint pen, perhaps?"

"Don't be snarky. I was just hoping we'd find out something more useful. We already know the two of them are an item."

I sighed. "True. We really need to question Jason right away. Should we knock?"

Her eyes widened. "And what? Just barge in, accusing them of murder? We're not the police, you know."

It was true. If I were Costa, I definitely would have been barging in. Unfortunately, people tended not to be so forthcoming. An idea popped into my mind. I rummaged around in my purse and pulled out a twenty.

"Here." I shoved it at Cheryl. "Go buy a cheap bottle of wine and bring it back. I'll stay here and watch the door, make sure they don't leave."

She stared at me, eyes narrowed, twenty-dollar bill clutched in her hand. "What are you planning, you minx?"

"Oh, you'll see." I waggled my eyebrows mysteriously. "Now hurry up before we miss our golden opportunity."

# # #

I gave an imperious rap on Piper's door, then stood back, wine bottles clearly visible to anyone peering through the peephole. The door swung open almost immediately, revealing Piper with disheveled hair and an awkwardly buttoned shirt. The woman had insanely long legs. I ordered myself not to be jealous. She stared at the wine bottles and then at me.

"Viola." She seemed genuinely surprised and not particularly alarmed. I wasn't sure if that was a good thing or a bad thing. "To what do I owe this pleasure?" I couldn't tell if she was being sarcastic or not.

I waggled the bottles in the air. "I wanted to stop by and say thank you. And bring you these. Wasn't sure what you drank, so one white and one read." I gave her my most beguiling smile.

A tiny frown line marred her otherwise perfect face. "Thank you? For what?"

"Well, you know, today. That whole ghastly episode." I shuddered dramatically. My mother claimed I was one of the most dramatic people she knew. She was one to talk. "You were just so kind. Very helpful." Piper had been no such thing, but in my experience, people generally thought they were better than they really were. If you told them they'd been kind, they'd take it. Even if they couldn't figure out what you were talking about. "I can't thank you enough. For being there. Taking my mind off the whole business. I thought we could share a bottle." I gave her a hopeful smile. "The three of us." I waved to Cheryl hovering in the background. She gave a little finger wave.

"Well, I do have a visitor..."

"Splendid!" I crowed, charging in through the open door before she could protest. "The more the merrier. Oh, Jason. How nice to see you again." I gave him a mournful look. "My condolences. You must be in shock. Here. Join us in some wine."

Jason, clad in a worn undershirt and unbuttoned khakis, stared at me with glassy eyes and a mouth slightly hanging open in shock. I could be a bit much when I wanted to—and oh, how I wanted to. I gave him a wide smile and cocked my hip in a sassy manner. "Corkscrew?"

Piper, after donning a pair of pajama pants beneath what was obviously Jason's shirt, obligingly found a corkscrew and four glasses while Cheryl made cheerful chitchat with Jason. The meaningless talk seemed to calm him down. He looked less like a rabbit in headlights and more like his old self. Not that I knew him that well, but I'd seen him around over the years, toddling behind Natasha like a good little minion.

I poured four generous glasses and held mine up in a toast. "To friends!" I declared cheerfully. "And living to fight another day."

Cheryl nearly choked on a mouthful of wine. Piper looked only mildly interested as she took a seat on the sofa, curling one leg under the other. Jason had gone white again.

"I...I'm really sorry to hear about wh...what happened today, Ms. Roberts," he stammered.

"Viola. And thank you."

"Terrible thing. Terrible. How could anyone do such horrible things? First Natasha," he seemed to choke a little on her name—whether from disgust or genuine sorrow, it was hard to tell. "Then this awful incident at the hotel. You could have *died*."

"True. But I didn't." I gave him a brave smile. "That's something to be thankful for."

"Too true. Too true." He swallowed an alarmingly large mouthful of wine.

"It was really scary," Cheryl was fully into her role now, relishing every minute. I was not the only one with a flair for the dramatic. "I mean, I only heard Viola scream, but Piper, you were closer. Surely you must have seen something." She widened her eyes in feigned innocence.

"No. Nothing," Piper muttered, nose buried in her wine glass.

"That's too bad," Cheryl said mournfully.

I gave her a look. Girl was laying it on a little thick. Fortunately neither of our suspects seemed to notice, even though Piper was probably one of the cleverest people I'd ever met.

"What did the police say?" Jason asked. "Surely someone called them."

"The police didn't say much," I admitted. "I doubt they think it's related." Liar, liar. "Just an accident."

He seemed to breathe easier. He took another deep swallow of wine, nearly emptying his glass.

"Although," I continued, watching him stiffen back up, "I do believe Detective Costa plans to question everyone again. Just in case."

Piper nearly dropped her glass. A few drops of wine spattered on her pajama pants. "You mean us?"

"I imagine so," I murmured taking a sip of wine. "After all, you're part of the investigation. Costa has to be thorough, I'm sure."

Jason was looking increasingly ill. "But we had nothing to do with this!" he wailed loud enough to wake the dead.

"Of course not," I soothed, reaching over to pat him on the forearm like an elderly aunt. "I mean, the fact Costa even suspects you is just ridiculous. Isn't that right?" I turned to Cheryl for confirmation. She gave it willingly, if perhaps a little overenthusiastically. "What we need to do," I continued, "is to show Costa that you had no reason to kill Natasha. Then I'm sure he'll cross you both right off the suspect list."

Jason sank into one of the kitchen chairs. "You think so?"

"Oh, I'm sure of it."

Piper stared moodily out the sliding glass door, beyond which the surf pounded against the sugar white sand. "That would be a relief," she finally admitted. "Not saying that...witch didn't get what she deserved, but we didn't do it."

"Piper," Jason admonished, "it's unkind to speak ill of the dead."

"Oh, get real, Jase." She whirled on him, her face an angry mask. "That woman made both our lives miserable, and you know it. It's a relief she's dead, but neither of us are killers."

"Okay, all right." I rushed in to soothe ruffled feathers. "Anyone who knows you knows that, but Costa is a stranger. He's just doing his job, so we've got to help move things along in the proper direction. Right?"

Everyone agreed.

"How?" Jason asked.

"Well, let's think." I tapped my chin, pretending to be in deep thought. "Why would Costa suspect you in the first place? Other than that they always suspect the spouse, of course. And, I'm sorry to point it out, but you were in the midst of a nasty divorce."

"I don't know why he'd suspect me," Jason wailed. "There's no reason—."

"Well, there was the fight," Cheryl pointed out helpfully as she grabbed a second bottle of wine and topped off her glass.

Jason looked blank.

"At the party," I nudged.

His face cleared. "Oh that." He waved his hand dismissively. "That was nothing. She was behind on her monthly payments. As usual. All part of the pre-divorce agreement. But it's nothing that wouldn't have been taken care of eventually. Just a game she loved to play."

Piper snorted, upper lip curled, but said nothing. I'd had no idea he was getting alimony, or whatever it was. I'd assumed he was flat broke. It wasn't surprising

Natasha had kept that hush-hush. She definitely wasn't the sort who'd like people knowing her almost-ex was getting a cut of her money.

"Okay, so the almost-ex-husband angle. They always think the ex has something out for the victim, right? So, like, would she have done something you might have wanted revenge for? In the eyes of the police, I mean."

"Of course not," he said. "Even if I was out for revenge, it would have been stupid of me to take it."

"Why's that?" Cheryl asked.

"Because I needed her alive if I wanted to keep getting alimony after the divorce was final. And believe me, they were very nice checks."

"All right, how about inheritance? The police would definitely look into that. Who inherited Natasha's money and book rights?"

"Oh, that all goes to her sister," Jason said with a wave of his hand. "She changed the will long before our marriage failed. I don't get a damn thing. See, I told you. Natasha was worth far more to me alive. Without her, I'm broke."

Chapter 12
Back in the Spotlight

"Well, there goes suspect number one," Cheryl said glumly.

"And number two," I agreed with equal gloom.

"Piper?"

"Exactly. Killing Natasha would have meant killing the goose that laid the golden egg. So to speak. With Natasha alive, Piper got to live off the money Jason was getting from Natasha every month. With her dead..." I shrugged.

"I see your point," Cheryl said morosely. "Now what?"

I sighed. "Let's take a walk along the beach. Clear our minds."

"Sounds good. As long as we don't find any bodies."

At the edge of the sand, we shucked our flip-flops and padded barefoot down the beach. The sound of the waves lulled me into something approaching a moment of Zen. Without thinking about it, I turned in the direction of the Don CeSar Hotel and the scene of my earlier near-meeting with the Grim Reaper.

Most people would probably be worried about that. Almost dying. Call me crazy. Call me stubborn. Call me out of touch with reality. But for whatever reason I wasn't afraid. Not of death. Not of whoever had tried to kill me. I was a little pissed off and determined to discover who the culprit was, but I wasn't afraid.

"We must be close," I mused aloud.

"To what?" Cheryl glanced around as if trying to figure out what I was talking about.

"To the identity of the killer, of course. To finding out the truth. Otherwise, why would someone try and kill me?"

"Because you're nosey." There was an edge of sarcasm in her tone.

I laughed. "It's true. But people don't generally kill other people just for being nosey. Not unless they have something to hide."

"I suppose you're right. Too bad *we* can't figure out how close we are."

I couldn't agree more. Clearly the killer was getting antsy, but the reality was I had no idea who he or she could be. It seemed I'd eliminated the most likely suspects. Of course, there was still Yvonne, the acquisitions editor. Not to mention, Avery Andrews, Natasha's biggest competition, and Greta Morris, Natasha's current PA, but I considered them not particularly likely. With Natasha's death, Greta was out of a job. Ditto Yvonne. Well, not out of a job, but she'd lost her biggest client. The only one who even vaguely benefited from Natasha's death was Avery, who now took the number-one romance spot at the publishing house. Romantic Press would be dumping all the marketing budget they'd spent on Natasha into Avery's books now, and that could only boost her sales even more. Yep, Avery had a lot to gain from the murder. I mentally added her to my list of people to be questioned. Also, I still needed to figure out who owned the bracelet I'd found and if it was important to the investigation or simply a coincidence. My gut was telling me there was no such thing as coincidence.

We drew abreast of the hulking pink giant that was the Don CeSar. It looked different from the beachside. Even more elegant and imposing. I noticed a large group of guests huddled around the beach access door. They seemed to be waiting for something. I frowned when I caught sight of a uniformed police officer guarding the entrance. Something was up.

"Come on." I nudged Cheryl. "Let's go check it out."

She groaned, but otherwise didn't protest, which I took for consent. Not waiting to see if she followed, I took off across the perfectly raked white sand toward the huddle of people. I quickly sought out the most gossipy-looking one of the group: an elderly gentleman with enormous white sideburns and beady, dark eyes that saw everything. He was the only one who'd been given a chair, which probably had a lot to do with the cane clutched between his gnarled hands. He looked ready to burst.

"What's going on?" I asked, breezing up like I belonged there. "Why aren't they letting us in?"

The old man's eyes twinkled with barely repressed excitement. "It's the police. They told us we couldn't go in. Things afoot."

I gave him a conspiratorial look. "What sort of things?" My blood zinged with excitement. Had there been a robbery or something?

The old man's smile broadened as if he held the best secret in the world. "You'll never believe it," he said. "This sort of thing never happens here. Not at the Don CeSar."

"What sort of thing?" I asked impatiently.

He waggled his eyebrows meaningfully. "Murder."

# # #

"This way." I waved Cheryl to follow me around the side of the building. I figured the police couldn't have every entrance blocked. There was always some side door or something. A service entrance, that sort of thing.

"Are you sure we should be doing this?" Cheryl asked, looking a little worried.

"Probably not. But a faint heart never solved a murder mystery."

"That's not how the saying goes," she said dryly.

I shrugged. "Hey, whatever works, right?"

With a glance over my shoulder to make sure nobody was watching—particularly the police—I crept around the side of the building, Cheryl hot on my heels. The way was dimly lit by ornate wrought-iron lamps and the pebbled walkway nearly overgrown with lush, tropical greenery. Although a narrow path wound its way down the side of the building, it was clearly not something the guests often used. Likely they stuck to the other side of the building with its enormous pool and varied selection of bars. We had it completely to ourselves. Even the police were absent.

The first side door we came to was one of those exit-only doors. Even if it hadn't been locked, we wouldn't have been able to get in. There was no handle. Hanging around until someone wandered out didn't seem like a good idea either. Who knew how long we'd have to wait?

We walked farther down the path, skirting stubby palm trees with branches that were in need of a trim and dodging spray from overly enthusiastic sprinklers. Finally we found another door. This one appeared like it might be an actual side entrance for employees or the odd guest seeking a smoke. I pushed gently on the crash bar and sure enough, it swung open.

"This way," I hissed.

"Why are we whispering?" Cheryl murmured back.

"Because we don't want anybody to hear us."

"What anybody?"

She had a point. There was no one around. No guests. No employees. And certainly no cops. Probably they were all over at the other side of the building where the excitement was, which was where I wanted to be.

The door led into a narrow hallway. Very bare and boring. Nothing at all like the opulent upstairs. Definitely a service entrance. I racked my brain trying to remember if this part of the building had been on the ghost tour, but I hadn't been paying any attention after my near-death experience.

On either side of the hall, doors led to various storage, janitorial, and laundry rooms. Up ahead I could hear the telltale crash and bang of pots and pans. We'd need to avoid the kitchen if we didn't want to have people questioning us. I figured I could claim I was a guest who got lost, but if they looked it up, they'd know I was lying. And Cheryl was a terrible liar. She'd look guilty the whole time.

Fortunately we found a stairwell before we reached the kitchen. It was right next to the bank of service elevators. I didn't dare take those. Who knew where they'd open up or who'd be waiting on the other side? No, the stairs were a better option.

The stairwell was one of those ominous places with ringing metal steps and lots of echoing concrete walls. Fluorescent lights flickered overhead turning skin sallow. It was exactly the sort of place I expected some evildoer to jump out of the shadows and attempt ghastly murder. However, we made it to the lobby floor unmolested.

There was no window in the stairwell door, so I pushed the door open a crack and peeked through. Cheryl crowded up behind me, trying to get a look.

"Would you stop?" I hissed.

"I can't see."

"Neither can I."

The door suddenly swung open, and I crashed face first to the floor, Cheryl landing on top me. We both let out unladylike squeals followed by *oomphs*.

A pair of scuffed, black leather shoes appeared in front of my nose. "Well, well. Ms. Roberts. And her sidekick. Why am I not surprised?"

I pushed dark locks of hair out of my eyes as I glanced up to find Detective Costa staring down at us, arms crossed over his broad chest. He did not look happy to see either one of us.

"Oh, Detective. Hi!" Cheryl said perkily, scrambling off me with a few well-placed jabs of her elbows—sharp elbows, at that. "How's it going?" I could tell her innocent tone did not fool Costa one bit.

I heaved myself to my feet a little more slowly than Cheryl had. In part because I'd been the one to hit the floor. In part because I was putting off dealing with Costa and his disapproval.

"Hello, Detective," I said coolly, brushing off my navy capris, though there wasn't a speck of dirt on them. The Don CeSar kept their floors pristine. "Fancy meeting you here."

Costa said nothing. He just tapped one foot on the marble floor, arms crossed over his impressive chest.

"What's going on?" I tried to peer around him, but he was a bit on the broad side, and all I could see were cops everywhere and a bit of crime scene tape fluttering in the wind from the open front door. "Having a party?" I laughed, but it came out a little strained.

"Are you investigating what happened to Viola?" Cheryl asked. I couldn't tell if she was playing along or if she was actually serious. I couldn't imagine Costa would care one whit about finding out who'd pushed me. More like he was wishing they'd finished the job.

He gave Cheryl an exasperated look. "I'm a homicide detective, Ms. Delaney. I'm not in the habit of investigating accidents."

Cheryl snorted angrily and shot Costa a glare. "That was no accident, and you know it. Otherwise, why would you have come out the minute you heard about it?" She arched one dark eyebrow and crossed her arms, mirroring Costa's stance. I was impressed. I didn't know Cheryl could have quite so much chutzpah in the face of such an imperious jerk.

"Be that as it may," he said imperturbably, "this investigation is none of your concern."

"What investigation?" I asked, ears perking up. "Are you telling me there was a murder here? It's related to Natasha's death, isn't it?" I watched his face closely; otherwise I might have missed the slight twitch of jaw muscle. "It is!" I crowed. "But how? Who is it? Who was murdered?"

Costa pinched the bridge of his nose between his thumb and forefinger. "Just go home, Ms. Roberts, and leave the investigating to the professionals."

"Can't go home," I said smugly. "I live in Oregon, and my flight isn't until Monday."

He literally groaned. I had to hold back a laugh.

"To your hotel, Ms. Roberts. Go back to your hotel."

"This is a free country last time I checked. I can stay here until you-know-where freezes over," I said even more smugly. Taunting the devil probably wasn't smart, but I was hoping that if I goaded him enough, he'd let slip some information useful to my investigation.

Costa looked ready to explode. "Ms. Roberts..." There was a warning edge to his tone. I figured I'd pushed his buttons hard enough for one night.

I held up my hands placatingly. "All right. I'll go. But at least tell me who died. Maybe I can help. I did find the first body, after all." I winced realizing I'd just reminded him of my suspect status.

"Believe me, I haven't forgotten." He lifted a hand and waved over a uniformed officer. She hurried to his side, eyes wide, body thrumming with excitement.

"Yes, sir?"

"Crowley, please escort these ladies off the premises. Make sure they get a car back to their hotel."

"Yes, sir!" Crowley's tone was a little perkier than I thought correct for a police officer. It was clear she was young and eager to please. Maybe I could use that to my advantage.

"This way, ladies." Crowley waved us toward the front entrance. Cheryl dutifully did as Crowley asked, but I lingered at the policewoman's side, keeping pace with her.

"Officer Crowley, is it?"

"Yes, ma'am."

I held back a wince at the "ma'am," reminding myself it was a Southern thing. It had nothing to do with my age. Much.

"How long have you been a police officer?" I gave her a wide-eyed, innocent look.

"A year and a half, ma'am."

"Wow! And here you are on a homicide already. How exciting! Not the person dying, of course," I rushed to add, "but it's kind of a big deal, isn't it?"

"It is quite an honor working with Detective Costa, yes." She practically beamed with excitement.

"I just ask because I'm a writer, you see. I'm always doing research for my novels. Police procedure is especially important to get right. You don't know how many readers email me with comments when I get something wrong!"

I left out the part about me writing Westerns and that the things I got wrong were usually historical details. Like the time I had the Pony Express operating in 1862 when it went bust in '61. You should have seen the outrage I got over that one. It wasn't even my fault. It was a typo, for goodness sake.

"You're a writer? That's so exciting! I always thought it would be fun to write novels. Maybe crime fiction or something like that." She grinned widely, revealing perfectly straight teeth which had obviously had some seriously expensive orthodontia.

"Oh, yes, so fun." It was. But it was also hard work. I didn't bother going into that. I needed information. "Is this your first homicide?"

She nodded. "I didn't even throw up."

My eyes widened of their own accord. I didn't have to feign surprise. "You saw the body?"

"First on the scene," she said proudly. She lowered her voice, "My cousin works here, so he called me. He knows I patrol the area."

"Gosh, that must have been shocking. Was it your first dead body? I would think I would pass right out cold." I gave a delicate shudder.

"I'm a police officer, ma'am," she said, puffing out her chest. "We don't pass out." She gave me a conspiratorial look. "Although my partner, Raston…he lost his lunch. And he's been on the job ten years!"

"Well," I said with approval, "we all know that women are the stronger sex."

She nodded in agreement. "You aren't lying."

"What was it like?" I asked. "I'm writing a crime scene next, you see." Liar, liar. "I've got to get all the details right. Was there blood?" By then we were at the curb waiting for the Uber. According to my app, I had three minutes to get all the information I could out of Crowley.

"There was blood," she confirmed. "A lot of it. Head wound. The medical examiner says she was hit on the head with something before she took a tumble down the stairs. Poor thing."

My ears perked up. Now that sounded familiar. At least the stairs part. We were passing a large grouping of police, behind them the yellow crime scene tape roping off the grand staircase. I managed a peek between all the muscled legs and torsos, but the body was already gone. I could still see the pool of blood where the victim fell, bright red against the white marble.

"She? The victim was a woman? Was she a guest?"

Crowley shrugged as she ushered me outside. "Not a guest here anyway. No one is sure who she was. Guess that's one for Costa to figure out." A silver car slid to the curb. "Here's your ride, ma'am. It was nice talking to you. Get home safe." The minute I was in, she shut the door firmly behind me. And that, as they say, was that.

Chapter 13
Into the Great Beyond

We entered the Fairwinds Resort lobby to find complete and utter chaos. Huddled groups of employees gathered around crying. Guests milled about, looking confused and anxious. The night manager was trying to calm everyone with limited success, and in the middle of it all, Kyle— the bartender and Natasha's lover—was arguing loudly with a female bartender.

"Oh, please," the woman shouted over a sobbing waitress, eyes snapping angrily. "You never loved her, Kyle. You ditched her as soon as that nasty woman showed up."

"You don't know anything, Becky." Kyle slammed a glass down on the bar so hard it cracked. "I loved her more than you could ever understand." And with that, he stormed out of the bar and across the lobby to disappear down one of the corridors. It was all very dramatic. A little too dramatic. I could only surmise that the "nasty woman" Becky referred to was Natasha. So, Kyle had a girlfriend before Natasha. Someone he'd dumped to be with the diva. Could it be the sobbing waitress?

I edged closer to the bar, dragging Cheryl with me. I eyed Becky, the female bartender. "Men, eh?"

She snorted. "You have no idea. He's a womanizing jerk, that one."

I nodded to the still sobbing waitress. "That his ex-girlfriend?"

"No, that's Tiffany, Andrea's best friend. Andrea was Kyle's ex-girlfriend."

I frowned. "Was?"

Becky leaned over the bar, voice low. "We just got word. Andrea was killed tonight. Isn't that sad?" She glanced over at Tiffany. "Sorry, better go calm her down before my boss freaks out."

As she walked away, I grabbed Cheryl's arm. "I think the dead woman at Don CeSar was Kyle's girlfriend."

She frowned. "Did you hit your head? Natasha's been dead for days."

"No, no," I said impatiently. "His girlfriend *before* Natasha. From the sounds of the argument he just had, I'm guessing he dumped whomever it was for Natasha. Now not only is Natasha dead, but so is the old girlfriend, Andrea." Which begged the question: why would someone murder both of Kyle's girlfriends? It was an odd coincidence, if you asked me. Vendetta maybe?

Cheryl frowned. "Are you sure?"

'Not one hundred percent, but pretty sure. Let's talk to Becky some more."

"Becky?"

"Bartender." I nodded to the woman who'd been arguing with Kyle. She was patting the tearful waitress, Tiffany, on the back and shoving tissues at her.

Cheryl perked up. "I could use a drink."

We sauntered over and took seats on two of the empty barstools just as Tiffany managed to get herself more or less under control. She hurried off with a sad wave to Becky. We ordered our drinks, the usual blackberry bourbon for me and wine for Cheryl. I glanced around casually.

"Can you tell us what happened?" I asked Becky. She looked to be about thirty and was on the slender side with a colorful full-sleeve tattoo of a dragon on her left arm. "It's just so…awful. I can't imagine how you all are coping."

"Some of us worse than others, as you saw. The police were just here," Becky said with a shake of her head. "They were trying to find next of kin for a body they'd found—all she had on her was her work ID."

"Which led them here," I guessed.

She nodded. "Turns out it was Andrea. She worked here. Poor thing." She sighed.

I clucked sympathetically. "That's so sad. Where did she work? Maybe we met her."

"I doubt it. Andrea works in the spa. She's a massage therapist, but she was off most of this week. It's just terrible. And after Kyle dumping her and everything."

"Oh, I'm so sorry. I feel badly for her family."

"Well, in this case I guess it's a good thing she doesn't have any. She was raised in foster care, I guess. No relatives to speak of." Becky shook her head, her face hardening in anger. "She was so young. So sweet. Nobody deserves to die that way."

"What way?" Of course, I'd already guessed, but I needed confirmation.

Becky leaned across the bar. "We're not supposed to talk about it, but it's just so shocking, you know?"

I nodded. "I get it. I promise, my lips are sealed."

"Well, according to Lyn, our assistant manager, the police say somebody hit her over the head and then pushed her down the stairs over at the Don CeSar. Isn't that awful? Poor kid." She shook her head.

"That's dreadful," I murmured. Maybe I shouldn't have been, but inside I was dancing. Because I now had confirmation that Kyle's ex-girlfriend, Andrea, was the murder victim at the Don CeSar. What she'd been doing there and why she'd been killed were questions that still needed answering, but I'd no doubt that somehow or other, Andrea's and Natasha's deaths were somehow related, and I was going to find out how.

# # #

I half expected Costa to show up at my room that night, pounding on the door and accusing me of murdering poor Andrea. That seemed to be his general *modus operandi*. After all, I was pretty certain I was still on his list of suspects for Natasha's death, and Costa wasn't a stupid man. He'd no doubt already figured out the two killings were related.

Instead, I had a rather rocky night's sleep, followed by a peaceful morning cup of coffee. I even made it to the first lecture of the day: *The Future of Historical Fiction.*

I know. Scintillating, right? And it was actually interesting, the little bits I heard as my mind wandered to other things. Like murder.

I'd already more or less cleared Kyle of Natasha's murder. That meant he was probably innocent of Andrea's, as well—*if* the murders were connected, as I believed. Still, I made a mental note to check if he had an alibi.

I was also certain that Jason and Piper were innocent of Natasha's murder, and they had zero reason to kill this Andrea girl. I'd need to check their alibis, too, though. Had to be thorough.

I still needed to talk to the other three suspects in Natasha's death: Yvonne, Greta, and Avery. Though I couldn't imagine why any of them would kill Andrea, a woman they didn't know. Unless Andrea knew something about Natasha's murder, of course. But what? Had she witnessed it? Or had someone told her something? I needed to find out more about this Andrea.

I decided the best way to find out more about the victim was to speak to her coworkers. So I promptly made myself an appointment at the spa for a massage. All in the name of research.

The resort spa was one of those soothing, Zen places with world music—the kind with pan flutes and whatnot— playing softly over the sound system and scented candles burning in every nook and cranny. The decorator was inordinately fond of seagrass baskets and blue paint. Everywhere I looked, things were painted in varying shades of blue, mostly of the sky and seafoam variety. Even the artwork—which was modern in the extreme—consisted of slashes and splashes of cerulean and sapphire.

I was greeted by a young woman wearing a baby-blue smock and a serene smile, who showed me to a curtained alcove where I could undress. I was given a matching powder-blue robe and a pair of spa slippers and paraded down a wide corridor into a treatment room with a massage table and more scented candles that were probably supposed to smell of the ocean, but really smelled like bathroom spray. And, you guessed it, blue everywhere.

The woman said in a soothing manner that I should disrobe and climb onto the table face down and that my therapist, Rose, would be with me in a moment. I nodded agreeably and, once she left the room, disrobed and climbed on the table. I was determined to enjoy this to the fullest. A massage while interrogating? Best multi-tasking ever.

The door opened, and I turned my head to watch Rose pad in. She was dressed in a blue smock like the first girl and had her sunset-red hair up in a sloppy bun. The kind that always looked so cute on someone like Rose, but made me look like a homeless person with bad fashion sense.

"And how are we today?" she asked in well-modulated tones. The sort of tones that made me want to ring a person's neck. Maybe Andrea had been killed by a client for being annoying. I smirked and told myself not to be an idiot.

"A little tense," I admitted. "It's been a long week. This spa comes highly recommended."

"Oh, that's lovely. By whom?"

"Someone who works here. Andrea something?"

Her face fell. "Oh, that's so sad."

"Sad?"

Her blue eyes widened innocently. "Didn't you hear? Andrea has passed."

I frowned and played dumb. "Passed what?"

"Into the Great Beyond."

I widened my eyes as if in surprise. "You mean she's dead?"

"Shhh. We don't like to use words of negativity here," she said serenely. "This is a happy place."

Actually, it was one step up from a mortuary, but to each her own. "Sorry."

"Now, why don't you relax so we can begin?" She rubbed some unscented oil in her hands and began smearing it on my back before gently kneading my muscles. I nearly groaned in delight. I really needed to get a massage more often.

In any case, massage or no massage, it was time to get to work. "Well, I'm really sorry. About Andrea, I mean. I didn't know her or anything, but she seemed really nice."

"Oh, she was lovely. The sweetest person," Rose assured me. "I'm certain her light will shine brightly upon us from the stars."

Alrighty then. "Of course," I agreed cheerfully. "But it's just so sad. She was so young. How did she die?" I moaned as Rose hit a particularly sore spot right below my right shoulder blade.

"Breathe deeply," Rose reminded me. I complied, hoping she'd say more. She didn't disappoint. "I really shouldn't be talking about something so negative," she said, "but it's shocking, you know? They say," she lowered her voice as if imparting a great secret, "that Andrea was murdered."

"Oh, that's ghastly," I agreed softly, voice barely above a whisper. "That poor dear. Why would anyone want to murder that sweet girl?" I knew nothing about Andrea except that Becky the bartender had liked her and Kyle had dated her, but I figured saying nice things about Andrea would get me far with Rose and her positivity.

She didn't disappoint. "Well, if you ask me, it's something to do with the murder of that writer lady."

"Natasha Winters?"

I could feel her shrug. "I guess so."

"What would Andrea have to do with Natasha's murder? Did they know each other?"

"I don't think so, but the night before she died, Andrea told me she knew something."

"About the murder?"

"Yes, I believe so."

"Knew what exactly?" I asked eagerly.

"She didn't say," Rose said.

Disappointment flooded me.

"But I'm guessing she knew something about the murder. Something she didn't tell the police. That would be just like Andrea. She doesn't like to get people in trouble." Her tone turned dark. "Even if they deserve it."

"You think she knew who the killer was?"

I felt Rose shrug again. "Who knows? And now she's gone, we'll never know, will we? Now, deep breath. Let's focus on you."

I got no more information out of Rose. But my mind was in a whirl. Andrea had claimed to know something about the murder, and now she was dead. The question was: what did she know? I needed to find out and fast.

Chapter 14
Checking the Angles

I came out of my massage feeling like melted butter. Relaxed didn't even begin to describe it. I was all ready to go park my backside in one of the beach cabanas—one of the ones that hadn't contained a dead body recently—when I found my pathway blocked by a grim-looking man in a rumpled suit.

"Detective Costa, good morning," I said brightly, glad I was wearing my sunglasses so he wouldn't see my death glare. "To what do I owe this pleasure?" I might have said it a little more sarcastically than necessary.

His eyes narrowed, and he glowered down at me like he'd very much like to handcuff me and throw me in a deep, dark hole somewhere. "I think you know why I'm here, Ms. Roberts."

"Enlighten me."

A muscle flexed in his jaw. "Why were you at the Don CeSar last night? The truth."

I shrugged and turned to pad in the opposite direction of the beach. I had no idea where I was going, but I wasn't going to stand there and let Costa get all up in my personal space, accusing me of things I didn't do. I was getting mighty sick and tired of it. "Cheryl and I were taking a walk on the beach last night. We saw a crowd near the hotel and were curious. That's all. Nothing sinister."

"You sure take a lot of walks on the beach," he said. I turned and slid my glasses down my nose to give him an exasperated look. "We're in Florida. On the beach. That's what people do. Especially after they've been sitting in lectures all day."

"I just find it interesting that you spent the afternoon at the hotel for a ghost tour and nearly managed to get yourself killed, only to turn around and return in the evening. Right after someone else is killed."

I snorted. "You actually think I'd be dumb enough to kill someone at the very spot I nearly got murdered? And on the same day no less?"

"In my experience, murderers often do dumb things."

I barked out a laugh. "Clearly, you haven't met any good murderers." Neither had I, as far as I knew.

"Are you admitting something, Ms. Roberts?"

I whirled on him. "Don't be an idiot," I snapped. "You know darn good and well I had nothing to do with either of the murders. And if you think I did, well, you've got fewer brains than I gave you credit for." Okay, so snapping at a homicide detective who suspected you of murder probably wasn't the best plan, but he was really getting on my last nerve.

"I don't suppose you have an alibi?" he snarled, his eyes shards of ice.

"Well, how do I know? When did Andrea die?"

"So you know the murder victim!" He all but shouted *Ah ha!* It would have been funny if I hadn't been so annoyed.

I rolled my eyes in exasperation. "No. I didn't. But this is a small island. Word travels fast. By the time we got back to the Fairwinds last night, everyone here had already heard the news. Believe me, I'd have to be stupid *and* deaf not to know who the victim was. Now, time of death?"

He sighed. "Ten minutes past seven in the evening."

"That's very precise."

"A guest heard a scream and, a moment later, saw the victim tumble down the stairs. So, yes. Very precise." He eyed me suspiciously, waiting to pounce on me for a weak alibi, no doubt.

"Well, if you must know, I was sitting in a lecture hall listening to the last talk of the evening. There were a least a hundred other people in there. I was sitting next to Cheryl the whole time."

"I see." Clearly he didn't think Cheryl was much of an alibi, but he couldn't argue with the other hundred-plus people who'd been sitting in that room. At least some of them would have seen me. I was not exactly easy to miss.

"Well, then, thank you for your cooperation, Ms. Roberts." He nodded, turned on his heel, and strode off abruptly, leather soles smacking on the concrete.

"Jerk," I muttered under my breath.

"I hope that wasn't aimed at me," a voice said cheerfully from behind me.

I whirled to find Lucas standing there in a pair of board shorts, flip-flops, and nothing else. It was a sight to see, believe me. My heart was doing ridiculous things in my chest. Like backflips.

"Oh, hi. How much of that did you hear?" I couldn't help the slight flush of embarrassment.

"Enough to know that you put that detective in his place," he said with a wide grin. "That man has been harassing you a little too much. And for no reason."

"He seems to think I'm a killer just because I found Natasha's body."

"That's ridiculous. And besides, you have an alibi for the second murder. Surely he'll take you off the list of suspects now?"

"I wouldn't bet on it," I said dryly. "I think the man is determined to find me guilty. And if not me, then Cheryl. In fact, I think he'd be happy to lock both of us up just on principle."

"I wouldn't worry about it," he said soothingly. "I've worked with a lot of police over the years, doing research for my books. He's just doing his job. He has to check all the angles, you know."

I sighed. "Yeah, I know. It's frustrating, though. Pompous jerk. Anyway, where are you headed?"

Lucas grinned that charming grin of his that made my internal backflips rev up a notch. "Thought I'd find a cabana, preferably minus a dead body, and relax for a bit. Want to join me?"

Did I? Be still my heart.

# # #

I gave a blissful sigh as I sank back into the shade of the cabana. White canvas flapped gently in the light breeze off the ocean. It was still humid as all get out and way too warm for my tastes, but the shady cabana kept the temperature somewhat bearable. The heat melted the tension, which Detective Costa had resurrected after my massage. I tried not to think of my gorgeous companion too hard…or the tension might return yet again—but in a good way, I supposed. Instead I pretended I was alone on a tropical island. All I needed was a fruity drink with an umbrella in it.

"So, you really are determined to see this thing through?"

Drat. There went pretending. I sighed and lifted my sunglasses to stare at Lucas. He was looking relaxed and delicious lounging on the cushions like a Greek god.

"Of course. Costa seems determined to find us guilty of something. I have to clear my and Cheryl's names before we end up locked away with the key tossed in the Gulf." The only thing we were guilty of was meddling. Which could be construed as being against the law. Sort of. I mean, if you wanted to look at it that way. But Costa was determined to be an idiot, so I had to save myself.

Lucas nodded. "All right. So what's next?"

I knew he wanted to help, but it was weird involving him. I barely knew the guy. Still, it might help to have someone besides Cheryl to bounce ideas off of. Plus I was pretty sure Cheryl was getting tired of my shenanigans. This might give her a break for a bit. Let her recover.

"Honestly? I'm not sure. Here's what I know." I gave him a quick rundown of what happened at the hotel the night before and what I'd learned about Andrea from Rose. "I need to find out more about Andrea. Like, did she have a new boyfriend? A best friend? Somebody she might have told what she knew about Natasha's murder or whatever it was she was hiding."

"Seems like a good avenue of investigation," Lucas agreed.

"And then there are the minor suspects."

He quirked an eyebrow. "That's a new one."

"Minor suspects are those that seem unlikely, but could have a motive for one or more of the murders."

"Like?"

I wiggled into a more comfortable position. I noticed his eyes strayed to my cleavage before politely glancing away. I wasn't sure if I was disappointed at his self-control or pleased that he was being such a gentleman. Maybe a little of both.

"Like Yvonne Kittering, for instance. On the one hand, the woman hated Natasha. Natasha made her life a living hell. Motive if I ever heard one. On the other hand, Natasha was her bread and butter. Without her, Yvonne doesn't have a career. Which, of course, is an even bigger reason *not* to kill her." I frowned. Logic was so annoying.

"What about Avery Andrews?" he asked. "Wouldn't Yvonne just pick up with her where she left off with Natasha?"

I was surprised Lucas knew so much about the romance world. Granted, there was likely some overlap with the way things were done with thrillers, but there were still a lot of differences. I shook my head. "Avery has a different acquisitions editor. Avery would either stay with that editor or go to one higher up the chain."

"And that wouldn't be Yvonne."

I shook my head. "Nope. Yvonne is out of luck unless she manages to find someone who can compete with Natasha's success and that's unlikely."

"Why?"

"Because Yvonne and the publishing house made Natasha. Three years ago, she was nobody. They literally created her success. With a new author, they'd have to start from scratch again. Why do that when they've got Avery already high in the charts? Throw some more marketing her way, and she'll be at least as big as Natasha, if not bigger. She's a better writer, after all. Plus she's nicer. Easier to work with."

"Natasha was a bit of a diva."

"That's a nice way of putting it," I said wryly.

He swung his feet to the sand. "Why don't you and I go question Yvonne? She may not be a good suspect, but I'll bet she knows something useful."

"Right now?" I asked, surprised by his eagerness.

He grinned that charming grin of his again. Was it hot out here, or was it just me? "You bet. Are you game?"

Was I ever.

Chapter 15
Getting On Top

We found Yvonne Kittering sitting at a table outside the Flying Fish, smoking like a fiend while swilling down a bottle of cheap red wine. She was already well on her way to being three sheets to the wind, and it wasn't even lunchtime yet.

"Hi, Yvonne," I said with a polite smile. "I'm Viola Roberts and this—."

She cut me off with a cloud of smoke, which caused me to cough. I made a production of it, which she ignored.

"I know who you are," Yvonne said. "Him, too." She shot Lucas a glare from her muddy-brown eyes as if he'd offended her by his very presence. "Come to gloat, I expect."

"Why would we do that?" Lucas asked soothingly, taking the seat across from her. I took the one between them. It faced the ocean, which was nice. Unfortunately it was closer to the cigarette smoke than I liked.

"Well, it seems to be what everyone else is doing. They're thrilled Natasha is dead. Ding, dong, the wicked witch and all that jazz," Yvonne said, waving her cigarette for emphasis. I tried not to cough up a lung as another cloud drifted my way. My allergies were going to run amuck any minute now.

Lucas shook his head and gave a sound of sympathy. "Some folks just aren't very nice."

Yvonne snorted. "You're telling me. And I worked for one of the nastiest ones in the business." She took another deep drag from her cigarette before splashing the last of the wine from the bottle into her glass. Then she pulled an industrial-size bottle of antacids out of her voluminous brown handbag and dumped a bunch of them on the table in front of her. "Natasha made my life a living hell. I suppose you know that." She took a drag, popped an antacid, and downed a mouthful of wine. "I'll bet the cops think I did it," she said morosely. Another drag, antacid, gulp of wine. She repeated the process as we chatted.

"Oh, I don't think they believe that," Lucas soothed. I was letting him roll with his "good cop" routine. He was good at it. Handling Yvonne like a pro. "I'm sure there are plenty of people who had motive to kill Natasha, but you're not one of them."

"You better believe it," she nodded emphatically, repeating once again the cigarette/antacid/wine process. She frowned when she found her glass empty. Lucas flagged down the waiter and asked for another bottle. Yvonne beamed at him, flashing slightly yellowed teeth. "Such a gentleman. Where was I? Oh, yeah, other people with motives." She leaned forward and whispered conspiratorially, "That Avery Andrews chick? Not quite as innocent and sweet as she'd like people to believe."

Lucas and I exchanged a glance. "No?" I asked.

She squinted at me as if just remembering I was there. "Nope. Definitely not. Do you know that she had an affair with Jason before he dumped her for Piper?"

I definitely hadn't known that. And neither had Lucas if the look on his face was anything to go by.

"I see that's news to you," Yvonne crowed just as the waiter returned with a fresh bottle of wine. She topped up her glass and took a deep swig, sighing with satisfaction.

"But if Jason broke up with Avery, wouldn't she have more motive to kill *him* than Natasha?" I asked. Yvonne didn't seem shy about spilling gossip about others, so I figured I didn't need to pretend to be anything but the nosey parker I was.

"Okay, here's the thing," she said, leaning one elbow heavily on the table. "Avery has a habit of wanting what isn't hers: husbands, book deals, whatever. Sure, she was angry as all get out over Jason leaving her, but she was angrier that Natasha got preferential treatment at Romantic Press. Plus, she already had her eyes on someone new by then, so losing Jason wasn't that big of a deal to her."

I wasn't sure where Yvonne was going with this, but she was certainly making Avery look guilty. It might sound silly to outsiders, but the book-deal thing could be the motive I was looking for.

"Word on the street is that Avery had already hooked up with the husband of another best seller. Drove her into a complete breakdown." Yvonne cackled with delight.

"Are you talking about Melisande Donovan?" I asked. She was the only best-selling romance author I knew who'd had a very public breakdown over her husband's affair, although the name of the woman involved had never been revealed.

"Oh, yeah," Yvonne said, slouching back in her seat, glass of wine clutched to her chest. "It was epic, let me tell you. Avery had a gag order slapped on her, which was why Melisande never mentioned Avery's name. Melisande still hasn't recovered. Poor dear." She seemed genuinely sorry for Melisande Donovan.

"I still don't see how that makes Avery a suspect," I said.

"I agree," Lucas nodded. "If Avery had been the victim, there are a few fingers we could point, but she seems to have no motive for Natasha's murder."

"I'm not done," Yvonne said smugly. "Two nights before Natasha's murder, I overheard a fight between her and Avery. Believe me, it was a doozy. There I was, minding my own business in the ladies room, and in walk the two of them. Started brawling like a couple of longshoremen."

"What were they fighting about?" I asked eagerly.

Yvonne's eyes glittered in unholy glee. "Turns out, Avery was trying to get her claws into Natasha's new man. Natasha wasn't pleased about it."

I blinked. "Avery wanted Kyle?"

"Is that the kid's name?" Yvonne shrugged. "All I know is threats were exchanged. And now one of them is dead." She waggled iron gray eyebrows. "What do you think of that?"

I thought it was highly suspicious. And I'd bet anything the police would, too. Except I had no intention of telling them. Not until I did a little more investigating myself.

# # #

"Let me guess." Lucas sounded amused. "We're off to question one Avery Andrews."

"Naturally. She just shot way up on my list of suspects."

"Ah."

I stopped to stare at him. "What? You don't think she could be guilty?"

He shrugged. "Anyone could be guilty, but as a motive for murder, trying to steal someone's boy toy is pretty weak, don't you think?"

I snorted. "Clearly you don't know women."

"Would you murder someone for trying to steal your boyfriend? Or worse, kill another woman to get her boyfriend?" he asked, seeming more interested in my answer than I would have thought.

"No," I admitted, "but believe me, there is a type of woman who would."

"And you think Avery is that type of woman?"

"That's what I'm going to find out."

"Mmm." The sound was noncommittal in the extreme. It made me want to slug him. Instead I gave an exasperated sigh and marched off in the direction of the main resort building. There were more lectures going on today, and Avery was giving one of them. Wouldn't hurt to hear what she had to say. Afterward I could question her. Subtly, of course.

The little computer screen outside the Seabreeze Suite listed Avery's name and the time of the lecture as well as the title: *Being Number One: Getting on Top and Staying There*. Interesting, seeing as how Avery had been number two until the day Natasha died. Fascinating foreshadowing there. Wishful thinking? Or had Avery already had a cunning plan to bump off her rival?

I slipped into the back of the room. Nobody paid any attention, their eyes were glued to the small stage up front. Couldn't say I blamed them. Avery was a stunning woman. More than that, she was charismatic without needing the diva attitude Natasha had been so infamous for.

Avery was wearing a bright-red dress that hugged her voluptuous form. Her mink-dark hair was swept up on her head in an elegant roll. She wore cute little black-rimmed reading glasses that made her look sexy rather than frumpy, and she clutched a laser pointer in one hand, which she used to highlight points on the overhead projection.

"Of course, I can't promise that what I did will work for you," she said with a warm chuckle that made everyone in the room smile, "but I can guarantee that if you do nothing, your results will be zero."

The room nodded as one. A few of the attendees scribbled madly in notebooks. Others tapped away at computer keyboards, trying desperately to capture Avery's wisdom in hopes that they could miraculously boost their own sales. Maybe they could. That wasn't why I was there.

As the class wound down, Avery assured the listeners that she would happily stay behind and answer questions, then she dismissed the class. She was immediately mobbed, most of them asking the same questions over and over again as if somehow that would produce some magical new information. It was a little like weight loss. Everybody wanted a so-called "perfect" body, but nobody wanted to put in the hard work. They were all looking for a miracle pill.

I waited, albeit somewhat impatiently, until the last person drifted away, leaving Avery alone to collect her things. Then I made my move.

"Interesting talk," I said cheerfully.

She arched a brow. "I noticed you missed most of it," she said. There was no accusation in her tone, merely observation.

"Ah, well, the beach called, you know."

She laughed. "Believe me, I get it. I'd have been out there, too, if I didn't have this talk to give." She said "talk" like one might say "circus" or "lunatic asylum."

"I'm sure everyone appreciated your time."

She sighed and tucked a laptop under one arm. "I've no doubt. I've also no doubt that most of them won't do a single thing I suggested and they'll get mad because I didn't fix things for them. I swear, this is the last time I do one of these talks." She laughed. "But then, I said that last year."

"I'm sure you helped someone in that crowd," I encouraged her.

"Hopefully. Plenty of room for all of us, I say."

That had me raising a brow. That was definitely not the impression I'd gotten from Yvonne.

"You're surprised by me saying that, aren't you?" Avery asked. "Well, it's true. Something Natasha never seemed to grasp."

"But now she's gone..." I let my voice trail off.

"And I'm number one. Believe me, the thought has crossed my mind. And Detective Costa's mind," she said dryly. She snagged her cobalt handbag off her chair. I had a moment of bag envy.

"Would you like to grab lunch?" I asked, hoping that she'd open up over food. Most people did, in my experience.

"That's sweet, but I already promised Piper Ross I'd have a lunch meeting with her. You know, talk over how she can help me grow my business. Now Natasha's gone, she can't get in the way."

"Really?" I was surprised she'd be interested in hiring Natasha's former assistant. "Not Greta Morris?"

Avery waved her hand dismissively. "Greta isn't the one that helped Natasha climb to the top. Piper is. Believe me, she's responsible for a lot more of Natasha's success than she's been given credit for."

"Really? I'd no idea."

"Exactly," Avery said darkly. "That was how Natasha preferred it."

"But what about, you know, Piper stealing Natasha's husband. Aren't you worried?"

She laughed. "I don't have anyone for Piper to steal. Besides, men don't get stolen unless they want to be. Believe me." She sounded like she spoke from experience. I couldn't help but think of poor Melisande Donovan.

"Well, good luck," I said cheerfully.

"I don't need luck, honey," Avery said with a smile. "I've got hard work and smarts on my side. Not to mention just enough talent to get by."

"That never hurts," I agreed, surprised at her candor. Most authors I knew liked to pretend they had no control over their success. Which was partially true, to a point. "Can I ask you something, though?"

"Sure. Fire away."

"There's a rumor that you and Natasha had a fight a couple days before she died. Over a man."

Her face went from open and bright, to dark and closed in a heartbeat. "That Yvonne Kittering has a big mouth."

"So you knew she overheard you?"

"Of course. And I didn't care. At least until Yvonne started spreading lies."

"Lies?"

Avery whirled on me, an angry flush staining her high cheekbones. "Do you honestly think I'd waste my time on a kid like Kyle?"

"To be honest? Not really."

"Exactly," she huffed. "I've got better things to do with my time than moon around with children. Besides, he's not my type."

"Then what were you arguing about?" I asked, baffled.

"I've never liked the way Natasha used people. I finally decided to tell her right to her face. Kyle may be a kid, but he deserved better than a woman like Natasha toying with his affections. Now, I've got to go. I'm already late." And with that, she sashayed out of the room leaving me standing there in a state of confusion.

Yvonne had painted Avery as a man-eating, power-hungry, do-anything-for-success type, but Avery hadn't seemed that way at all to me. She'd seemed genuine, normal, and a champion for the little guy. She was back to being dead last on my suspect list, and I no idea where to go from there. I wondered if Costa was as frustrated as I was.

Chapter 16
The Last Testament

There was one last person on my list of suspects which I'd yet to question: Greta Morris, Natasha's current personal assistant. Well, current until Natasha wound up dead on the beach, anyway. I decided to drag Lucas along. He seemed to have a way with middle-aged ladies. I cringed a little at the thought that I was now a middle-aged lady. That just didn't seem right. When had that happened? I heaved a sigh.

"Penny for your thoughts?" Lucas asked cheerfully. Drat the man anyway. Why was it that middle-aged men didn't get a bad rap? In fact, they generally seemed more desirable. More secure. More stable.

"Believe me, they're not worth it." I was this side of grumpy. Maybe I needed more coffee. Or a very large bar of chocolate.

We found Greta Morris in the coldest corner of the lobby, her blond hair, liberally streaked with gray, pulled back in a severe bun. She was bundled up in a woolly sweater which was an unfortunate shade of grayish-pink—I believe they call it crepe. It clashed with the woman's rather florid complexion and did no favors to her figure, making her look exceptionally lumpy. Admittedly, it was absolutely frigid in this particular corner of the lobby, but Greta's enormous sweater seemed like overkill. Still, this corner was also possibly the quietest, and Greta had her nose buried in her e-reader. It had a pink cover a shade brighter than her sweater. The woman must really love pink.

"Greta Morris?" I asked as if I didn't already know who she was. She blinked up at me through watery eyes. I noticed her nose was a bit red, and she clutched a tissue in her hand. Was she crying over poor Natasha? Or perhaps she was getting a cold. They seemed to be running rampant through the ranks of the NWA writers. Going from heat to cold every fifteen minutes had a habit of lowering one's immune system. So far, I'd been lucky to avoid it.

"Yes?" she blinked at me from behind thick lenses. She was pretty much the exact opposite of Piper: frumpy, not particularly attractive, and at least two decades older. Probably the exact sort of person I would have hired if my first PA ran off with my husband.

"I'm Viola Roberts." I didn't stick out my hand, not wanting her germs, but offered her a warm smile.

"Oh yes. I remember."

"And this is..."

"Lucas Salvatore," she breathed as if suddenly being confronted by a living god.

I resisted an eye roll, barely. "Erm, yes. You know his work?"

"But of course," she said eagerly, setting down her e-reader. "Sir, I can't tell you how many of your books I have enjoyed. I'm always up until at least four a.m. reading." She giggled like a schoolgirl, her cheeks pinkening even more.

"You just made my day. And call me Lucas." His voice was a low rumble. I shot him a glare. He was going a bit overboard on the sexy-writer thing.

His words made her giggle and blush some more, which was really unfortunate. The blushing, I mean. If her complexion had clashed with her outfit before, it did doubly so now. I tried not to be judgy, but pink was the last color poor Greta should be wearing. But if it made her happy...

"What are you reading now?" I asked with genuine interest.

She sighed. "Natasha's last book. The one we were working on before...well, you know." I nodded. "The publisher is still going to release it, so they've asked me to send them the files. I figured I might as well read it first. So emotional. So moving."

I frowned. Natasha's books were about as emotional as a donut. Scratch that, donuts elicited more emotion. Like that time when my local donut shop gave me a bacon maple donut instead of a regular maple bar. Trust me when I say bacon does not belong on a donut. Serious emotion happened there.

"Er, you mean because she died?" I asked, finding myself swimming in unfamiliar waters.

"Oh, no, the story really is moving. Unlike anything she's ever written before." Greta gave a surreptitious look around the lobby. "Let me tell you, I don't know how she had the following she did. Mediocre, if you ask me, but my job was to assist, not judge. This one, though…" She picked up the e-reader. "It's not like the others. This one is filled with passion and empathy." She gave me a funny look before stating awkwardly, "If I didn't know better, I'd have thought someone else wrote it."

# # #

"Ah, ha!" I said as I dragged Lucas outside into the muggy air.

"What 'ah ha'?" He asked in genuine confusion. I got it. He'd been too busy flirting with Greta to notice what I had noticed.

"Did you hear what Greta just said? How different that last book is? That if she didn't know better, she'd have thought Natasha didn't write it?"

"But Greta claims Natasha *did* write it. That she saw her working on it."

"Yeah," I admitted, "there is that. But she had a funny look on her face when she said it. What if Natasha was faking? It would be easy enough to copy and paste a block of text, then add a few words when the assistant walks in, so it looks like you're writing."

"But from where would she have got the manuscript?" he asked.

I frowned, nibbling on my thumbnail. "That's where I'm stumped."

"Anyway, I think you can strike Greta off the short list. She seemed surprisingly happy working for Natasha despite everything."

He was right. Greta had clearly been so grateful for the work, she hadn't minded Natasha's abuse. In fact, she'd gushed over the woman. Unless she was the world's greatest actress, she was telling the truth. After all, she'd been honest about Natasha's work. But what if she'd found out the truth about the new manuscript? Whatever truth that was.

Still, I couldn't imagine Greta plunging a dagger into Natasha's back. Kitchen knife. Whatever. Point was, I wasn't sure she was strong enough. Plus she was a lot shorter than Natasha. Not that I'm an expert or anything, but the angle of the knife suggested someone closer to Natasha's height.

"Okay, so Greta is off the list, but I still want to know who wrote that book. If it's as meaningful as Greta says, there is no way Natasha wrote it. She had to have stolen it from someone, and I'm pretty sure Greta knows it."

"Couldn't Natasha have had hidden depths you just don't know about? A secret yearning to write something deep."

I snorted with laughter. "Natasha? I take it you never met the woman."

"Only at the party."

"Well, let me assure you, I've known Natasha a long time. The woman was about as shallow as they come."

"Are you certain? After all, most people are multi-faceted. There could be more to her than you know."

I glared at him. "Whose side are you on anyway?"

He smiled. "The side of truth."

I sighed. He had to go and be all noble. "All right. I get it. I'm being judgy. But seriously, Natasha once told me something that has always stuck."

"What's that?"

"That she would do anything, even sell her own mother, to stay on top."

He gave me a look. "Are you sure you're not exaggerating?"

"I wish. You see, I made the mistake of asking her how she did it. Wrote so many books that readers love. You know what she said? She said that readers were intrinsically dumb and that if you just spoon-feed them what they want over and over, they'll eat it up. That she basically didn't give a fig for the craft or even about telling a good story, but rather cranking out more of the same. She said if she did that, she'd always be on top."

"I take it you don't feel the same," he said.

"Good grief, no. I can't speak for anyone else, but my readers are smart, savvy people. They're intelligent and educated. If I'm not keeping it fresh, they let me know. If I screw up the historical facts, they let me know. And I appreciate that. Keeps me honest and on my toes."

He nodded. "I get it. I have many readers like that. I once used the wrong caliber weapon, and believe me, I got lots of nasty emails educating me on my mistake." He laughed, clearly unoffended by any rudeness. "I won't be doing that again in a hurry."

"Exactly," I agreed. "You and I care about our readers. We care about our work, but Natasha cared only about winning. She wasn't the sort of person who would take a risk and write something so different from her usual trope."

"How are we sure it's that different?"

"Trust me, if it made someone cry, it's different," I said dryly.

"I'll take your word for it."

"Maybe if I could get my hands on a copy, I could figure out who actually wrote it," I mused. "Then maybe we'll have a new suspect."

The devilish grin flashed across his darkly handsome face. "Leave it to me."

"What? You got some special super powers I don't know about?"

Laughter was his only answer.

Chapter 17
Ghosts of the Past

"Viola Roberts!" a strident voice boomed across the lobby. Startled, I glanced up from my tete-a-tete with Lucas to find Maggie and Lu striding toward us.

"Ladies," Lucas said with his usual suavity.

"Good. Caught you," boomed Maggie, ignoring Lucas completely.

"How can I help you ladies?" I asked.

Lu beamed at me, but said nothing. Maggie continued at the top of her voice. "Party. Tonight. All the best people. Be there." She shoved a handwritten note in my hand. There was an address and time. Nothing more. "Bring that skinny friend of yours."

I frowned. "Cheryl?"

"Yep. Funny girl, that. Like her immensely."

"Sounds fun," I agreed. "We'll be there."

"And bring that one." She stabbed a finger in Lucas's direction.

"Ah, sure," I agreed.

The two older women started to turn away when Lu suddenly turned back. "I think you might find this of interest," she said in a soft Southern drawl. I stared at her in surprise. I was pretty sure this was the first time I'd heard her speak.

"Um, what?" I asked.

"I just overheard two of the maids talking about the dead girl."

"Natasha?"

"No." Lu shook her head. "The other one."

"Andrea? The girl from the spa?"

She nodded, pink, glittery Eiffel Tower earrings swinging wildly. "I heard one of them say she had a boyfriend."

"You mean Kyle? The bartender?"

"The same one Natasha was hanging around with? That's the one. I guess you already know." Lu looked disappointed I'd already heard her juicy new.

"Yeah. I heard last night. Crazy, isn't it?"

"Come on, Lu." Maggie grabbed her arm and gave it a tug. "That's enough gossip for one day. See you tonight." She gave a vigorous wave and then strode off, Lu trailing behind her.

"Well, that's interesting," Lucas said.

"You're telling me. Now all we need to do is find Kyle. We've got another suspect added to the list." Which, of course, was turning into a problem. Because I was finding a whole lot of suspects and not nearly enough answers.

# # #

"Are you sure I look all right?" Cheryl asked, fussing with the hem of her navy sundress. It fell to her knees, showing off her long legs. Simple silver sandals matched her jewelry. "This isn't very fancy."

"You look great," I assured her. "Stop worrying." I didn't bother to point out that everyone would be so busy staring at me, they wouldn't notice her elegant shift.

That may have sounded arrogant, but that was not really how I meant it. I bought the maxi sundress on a whim because it was bright and cheerful and I'd been doing some online shopping on a gloomy Astoria day. The dress turned out to be a lot brighter than it seemed on the computer screen. I'd nearly sent it back, then figured what the heck? I was headed to Florida, after all. The eye-searing coral and turquoise certainly stood out and, when paired with matching coral shoes, made a statement of epic proportions.

Sure enough, the moment we stepped onto the terrace, every eye swiveled toward me. I was hard not to notice. Which may have subconsciously been my point in keeping the dress.

The party was at the home of a friend of Maggie's and was situated on one of the many canals of St. Petersburg. It was a nice mix of elegant and relaxed with a massive terrace containing a small pool and a fire pit, unnecessarily lit on the hot Florida night. In my opinion, they should have had the party indoors in the air conditioning. Still it was a lovely spot, palm trees waving gently in the sunset.

"Viola! You made it!" Maggie's voice boomed across the terrace, setting off another round of staring. "And Cheryl. Lovely. Come on over. Get a drink."

Who was I to ignore such a command? With hibiscus martinis in our hands, Maggie and the ever-present Lu dragged us around the terrace making introductions. From industry professionals to other authors, Maggie seemed to know everyone. We weren't even halfway through before my head went fuzzy from all the input, and I could only smile and nod.

"And you know Lucas Salvatore, of course," Maggie boomed.

I sure did, although I might not have recognized him. He was wearing light khaki pants, flip-flops, and a flowery Hawaiian shirt, of all things. Mirrored aviators hid his eyes, and he leaned one hip casually against the bar, a sardonic smile on his handsome face. It was as if the guy I'd gotten to know had disappeared, and the famous author had appeared in his place. I wasn't sure I liked it.

"Ladies." He straightened and bowed over our hands in a ridiculous European manner. Not that it would have been ridiculous on an actual European, but in this setting, it felt contrived. He held on to my hand a little longer than necessary. I jerked it back, resisting the urge to smack the back of his hand like an old-fashioned school marm.

If I expected Cheryl to swoon over the royal treatment, I was disappointed. Her focus was on the other side of the pool. I squinted at the group standing there. There were a couple of female reps from one of the booksellers, neatly turned out with polished coifs and perfectly pressed skirt suits. How they didn't melt in this heat was beyond me. Around them hovered half a dozen authors, all vying for attention. One hung back from the group, obviously wanting to talk to the reps, but uninterested in playing sycophant. He wasn't terribly tall or super buff, but he was cute. He seemed a little shy, but stood his ground. I had no doubt that was where Cheryl's mind was. I couldn't remember meeting him, so I leaned over to Maggie.

"Who's that?"

Maggie turned toward the group, pineapple earrings swinging wildly. "The quiet one? Max Force. Not his real name, I'll bet money. Good choice, though. Writes crime novels."

I'd heard of Max Force. He was nothing like I imagined—my imagination tending toward brawny, retired cop. I nudged Cheryl. "Go talk to him."

She blushed furiously. "I couldn't."

"Sure you could," Maggie said with her usual subtlety. "He's single. Straight. Makes good money. Decent sort. You could do worse."

I nearly sputtered with laughter. "See? Maggie's seal of approval." I glanced at Lu who beamed and nodded. "Lu's, too." I gave Cheryl a little push. "Go get 'im, Tiger."

Cheeks still burning, Cheryl made her way around the pool. She hesitated a moment, but then Max glanced over at her. It was a whole *their eyes locked and the world stopped* moment. I couldn't have written it better myself. Leaving the two to their own devices, I turned back to Maggie, Lu, and, yes, Lucas.

"So," I said, eyeing him. "Would the real Lucas Salvatore please stand up?"

Maggie howled with laughter. Lu giggled, her eyes sparkling behind her red-rimmed glasses. And I swear Lucas actually snorted. With laughter.

"Ah ha!" I crowed. "I knew this one was a big, fat fake."

"You caught me," he admitted. "Truth is, people expect a certain sort of behavior from Lucas Salvatore."

"And you're happy to give it to them."

He shrugged. "Don't you find the same?"

I mulled it over. "Suppose so. I mean, people expect me to be perky and bubbly and obsessed with hot men."

He laughed. "Aren't you?"

"She's got the perky and bubbly down," Maggie said wryly.

I wasn't sure about that. "I do post a lot of half-naked men on social media," I admitted. "Usually cowboys. My readers have come to expect it."

"Exactly. As my readers expect a certain mysterious aloofness from me."

I gave him the eye. "Yeah. Good luck with that."

Lu let out a gasp, and Maggie swung toward her. She made her own sound of shock, so Lucas and I glanced over to where they were looking. Standing across the terrace was a woman of about seventy, although well preserved. She wore a flowing white pantsuit thing with gold high-heeled sandals and a matching white and gold turban on her head. She looked like a movie star from the seventies or something.

"Who is it?" I asked Maggie.

"Our nemesis," she hissed.

"You guys have a nemesis?" I asked, more than a little surprised. Maggie seemed the type to steamroll over anyone who tried to get in her way, and Lu wouldn't hurt a fly. I couldn't see anyone not liking her.

"You had Natasha. We have Veronica Dunham."

"That's Veronica Dunham?" I hissed. She was only one of the most famous historical romance writers in the history of historical romance. She was more or less the American answer to Dame Barbara Cartland. In her day, she'd churned out at least two romance novels a month. Her books could be found everywhere: from airport lounges to dollar stores. She'd made a veritable fortune before disappearing from public view. She hadn't been seen nor heard from in years. "I thought she was dead."

"Unfortunately, she's very much alive," Maggie said dryly. "And she's been talking making a comeback. She should have stayed retired." Her tone was nearly a growl.

I glanced at Lu. "What the heck did Veronica do?"

Lu's eyes glittered with excitement at knowing a piece of gossip Maggie was clearly reluctant to share. "She stole Maggie's work *and* her first husband."

Crikey. Just like Piper stole Natasha's husband, Jason. I swear writers do drama like nobody else. Not even soap-opera actors.

"Good riddance," Maggie muttered. Her gimlet eyes laser-focused on Veronica who was swanning down the steps in a way that made Natasha seem like an amateur in the diva business.

"Oh, do tell," said Lucas languidly, back to his author persona, it seemed. "It sounds juicy."

Juicy? "Yeah, spill. Maggie writes mysteries, not romances."

"Ah, that's what *you* think." Lu seemed to relish her sudden moment in the spotlight. "Once upon a time, she was poised to become the Next Big Thing in romance."

I stared at Maggie, my eyes wide with surprise. "You?" I just couldn't see the brusque, straightforward woman writing romance.

Maggie flushed bright red. "Hey, I enjoy romance as much as the next person. And I'd have done well in it if it hadn't been for Miss Diva over there."

"They'd been good friends since high school," Lu continued as if she hadn't been interrupted. "We all were. But when Maggie married her high school sweetheart, the two stopped speaking."

"Why?" Lucas and I asked together, now on the edge of our seats.

Maggie growled. Lu was downright giddy. "Because Veronica had always had a crush on him. She even tried to steal him away during senior prom. It didn't work. Then."

"Yeah, he waited until after we had four kids and a mortgage to play the jackass," Maggie snapped.

Lu giggled. "It's true! He made a right fool of himself mooning over That Woman." She said it as if

"That Woman" was a long-standing term for Veronica. No doubt it was.

"So, what happened?" I begged, watching Veronica sashay across the terrace toward a group of reps who seemed rather stunned at her appearance.

"I can't believe Cat invited That Woman," Maggie hissed.

"You know how Veronica is," Lu reminded her.

"Well, Cat should have warned me."

We all made sympathetic noises, but Lucas and I were more interested in the story. "Come on, Lu," Lucas said, dropping his author persona and returning to the more interesting man I was familiar with, "spill...more."

"All right!" she laughed. "Maggie and Bill had been married for ten years, and Maggie had just finished her first novel when Veronica came back into our lives. She acted like nothing ever happened. She was always bringing people expensive gifts, taking us out to lunch, throwing parties. You see, turns out she'd gone off and married some man thirty years her senior. A very *rich* man. When he died, he left her everything. Believe me, it was a lot."

"Wow," I said. "Why did she come back if she was so rich? She could have gone anywhere. Done anything."

"True," Lu said, "but some people get stuck at some point in their lives, and they can't move on. I suspect that Veronica was stuck on besting Maggie. But she covered it up well."

"Boy, did she ever," Maggie muttered.

"What'd she do?" I asked, trying to hurry the story along. I wanted the juicy bits.

"She acted interested in my writing," Maggie said. "So I showed her the manuscript." Her expression darkened. "The only copy."

I could see where this was going. And it wasn't good. That would have been years before the advent of soft copies and emails. Likely, the single hard copy would have been Maggie's only proof she'd written the thing.

"I'm guessing she monkeyed with it. Made it look like she wrote it," I said.

Maggie nodded. "You'd be right." "Veronica took it to a publishing friend in New York and got it into print under her own name before Maggie even knew what happened," Lu said.

"Lesson learned," Maggie bit out. "Should have kicked her narrow backside when I had the chance."

"You should have sued her," Lucas said.

Maggie shrugged. "I had no proof. I was out of luck."

"And your husband?" I asked.

"Darn fool fell head over heels." She shook her head. "Was gone before I knew what happened." Then she grinned evilly. "Veronica made him miserable. Tried to come back. Turned him down flat."

"Where is he now?" Lucas asked.

"Heart attack. Five years ago."

"Oh, I'm sorry," I said, feeling awful for Maggie.

"Don't be. Got what he deserved. Me? I made more money writing mysteries than I ever would have romances." She seemed fine with it, but I wondered if she really was. That was a hard thing, having a friend steal your work…and your man.

Something clicked. If Greta were to be believed, Natasha stole someone's work. And I doubted it was a stranger. I had a feeling whoever it was had been close to Natasha. But whom? Boy, did I want to see that manuscript.

Chapter 18
To Catch a Thief

The party went late, but I begged off around eleven. This whole adventure was making me tired, what with the jet lag and the murders and whatnot. Cheryl happily stayed behind to hang out with Max. I wondered wearily if I was seeing a romance in the making. Maggie and Lu stayed at the party, too. Maggie wanted to see what her archenemy was up to, and Lu was keeping an eye on Maggie "in case she goes postal." Lucas was nowhere to be seen. Schmoozing in his author persona, no doubt.

It was nice to get my pajamas on, take off my makeup, and curl up in bed with a good book. For once I needed the quiet. I was feeling a little overwhelmed by everything.

I hadn't been in bed long when there was a knock on the door. "Do you know what time it is?" I snarled without getting up.

"Yes. But I think you'll find it worth your while."

Lucas Salvatore. With a growl, I tossed back the duvet, climbed out of bed, and jerked open the door. "This had better be good."

Gone were the khakis and Hawaiian shirt. He was in a pair of worn jeans that fit him like a glove and a soft, gray t-shirt. Frankly, he looked good enough to eat.

"Believe me, it is." He held up a thumb drive.

I frowned. "What's that?"

"Natasha's last book."

"How the heck did you get that?" I asked, dragging him inside.

He laughed. "Hey, I have my ways. I just had a nice chat with Greta, and she agreed to let me see the manuscript, but only if it couldn't be traced back to her. Hence the drive."

"Gimme." I snatched it from him and padded down the hall to the living area. Turning on the light, I flipped open my laptop and inserted the thumb drive. I quickly opened the files. The only thing on the drive was a single manuscript titled *Lovers Lost*.

"Doesn't sound terribly exciting," I said with a frown.

"Greta assures me it is."

I started reading the first chapter, Lucas leaning over my shoulder to read along. I was keenly aware of his presence. The way he smelled, the heat coming off his skin. If I wasn't careful, I could easily fall for Lucas Salvatore. And wouldn't that be silly? I didn't have time for romance. Especially what would no doubt be a long-distance one. Besides which, I was still a murder suspect.

After a few pages, I knew what I was reading. "There is no way Natasha wrote this," I said. "I've read her drivel." I considered it a good policy to stay on top of the best-sellers in my genre. "This isn't even close to her style. The phrasing. The words the author uses. It isn't Natasha."

"Do you recognize it?"

"No," I admitted, "but I think I know who will."

"Who?"

"The one person who knows Natasha's writing better than anyone."

"Piper Ross," he said.

I nodded. "Do you think maybe this is what I saw Yvonne and Greta arguing about? Surely Yvonne knew this was a plagiarized book. She worked with Natasha too long to be fooled. Perhaps Greta was uncomfortable with it or something."

He shrugged. "Makes as much sense as anything. Maybe you'll know more once you talk to Piper."

I cleared my throat and folded my hands primly on the table, suddenly nervous. "It's a little late to go banging on her door. How about a glass of wine?"

His grin widened. "Sounds like a great idea."

I pulled a bottle of cabernet sauvignon from the cupboard. I'd picked it up at the local grocery store the day I arrived. Not my favorite label, but then I preferred Pacific Northwest wines, snob that I was. I made short work of the cork and, after pouring out two glasses, joined Lucas in front of the Juliette balcony overlooking the sea. It was a perfect night: warm, but not overly humid for once, with a nice breeze coming off the ocean.

"Are you always this determined?" he asked, eyes dark pools in the moonlight. He leaned against the wrought-iron railing, the wind teasing his dark hair. Man, I wanted to run my fingers through that hair. I bet it was soft as silk.

I gave myself a mental shake. "What do you mean?"

"I mean this murder thing. You seem almost obsessed with it."

I shrugged. "Wouldn't you be if someone accused you of being the killer?"

"I suppose I would be, but I admit I'd probably leave it to the professionals. They'd figure it out eventually."

I snorted. "Maybe, but I'm not going to count on it."

"So are you this determined in other aspects of life?"

I thought about that a moment. "I suppose. I mean, my writing certainly. I always wanted to be a writer ever since I was a kid, but I never did much about it. Not for years. Once I decided to go for it, I did. Full out, no holds barred. I figured if I was going to try it, I was giving it everything or nothing. So I gave it everything."

He nodded. "That I can understand. What about...relationships?"

I gave him a sideways glance. What was he getting at? "Depends on the relationship, I guess. Some are easy. Like Cheryl and me. We've been friends for years. Get on like a house afire. It's easy. Others, not so much. Some really aren't worth the effort."

"Sounds like you speak from experience."

"I do," I said, but my tone put an end to that part of the conversation. He obviously got it because he changed the subject.

"How'd you two meet? You and Cheryl."

I grinned. "Writers' conference in Vegas. Oh, we'd talked online for a couple years before that. One of those writers' groups where people try to encourage each other and exchange information and whatnot. But Las Vegas was the first time we met in person."

"Sounds like a story."

I laughed. "Oh, it is." The shenanigans of that week were legendary in our small circle of writerly friends. "But it's a story for another time, I think," I said, glancing at my watch.

"Sorry." He set down the empty wine glass. "I didn't mean to keep you up so late."

"No worries," I said with a smile. "I just want to attend the first class of the morning. It's on what's hot in historical romance. Eight o'clock comes rather early."

"Sounds right up your alley," he said with a smile.

I walked him to the door feeling suddenly fidgety and awkward. My heart was pounding in my throat, and I felt overly warm for the chill of the air-conditioned room.

"I'll see you in the morning, Viola," Lucas said, tucking a lock of hair behind my ear. I shivered as his fingertips skimmed the side of my neck. He leaned down to brush his lips across my cheek, only I started and his mouth landed on mine instead. I could have melted right there on the spot. "Sorry," he murmured, pulling back. Was it my imagination or was his move on the reluctant side?

"Uh, don't be," I said, trying to get my brain back in gear. His kiss had left me...breathless. Fuzzy headed. And a little dizzy. And it had only been the merest brush of lips. What if he kissed me properly? Talk about nuclear meltdown.

He gave me a lopsided grin. "Tomorrow."

I nodded, and he was gone. Out the door and melting into the night.

# # #

I spent the rest of the night tossing and turning, unable to think of anything but the sort-of kiss between Lucas and me. It had been a long time since a man had affected me like that. I wasn't sure how I felt about it. I was used to being alone. Used to making my own decisions. I wasn't sure I wanted a man mucking up my life.

I told myself not to be ridiculous. After all, Lucas hadn't even meant to kiss me on the mouth. He'd meant to kiss my cheek, and cheek kisses didn't mean anything. I was getting way ahead of myself.

By five a.m., I finally gave up and took a quick shower, downed a cup of coffee and a carton of yogurt, and threw on another maxi dress. This one in more demure shades of brown and teal. Then I made my way to the resort business center. It was a matter of minutes to plug in the thumb drive and print off a few pages of the manuscript.

By the time I finished that, it was only seven o'clock. The class started at eight. Would it be considered rude to visit Piper this early in the morning? Probably, but frankly, I didn't care. I was on a mission!

Fortunately, I needn't have worried about waking Piper. I found her at the lobby bar, working on a massive mug of steaming hot coffee. She looked as sleep deprived as I felt.

"No Jason today?" I asked cheerfully as I slid on the stool next to her. I indicated to the bartender that I'd have what Piper was having.

"It's not like we're attached at the hip," she growled, not looking at me. There were tight brackets around her mouth which I hadn't noticed before. I could see dark circles under her eyes and the clench of jaw muscles.

Okay. Not a morning person, then. Or maybe something else was going on.

"You going to the eight o'clock?" I asked.

She grimaced. "I'm not here for the conference. Or didn't you realize that?" Her tone was snippy. I resisted the urge to snipe back.

"Ah. Jason brought you as a…ah…companion. Maybe to make Natasha jealous?"

"Idiot. Why are men always such idiots?"

I didn't answer that. For one, I figured she wasn't looking for an answer. For another, I didn't think she'd much like what I had to say on the subject.

"Piper, I have a favor to ask you."

She gave me a glower. "Seriously?"

"Seriously." I slid the pages I'd printed across the bar. "I was given a copy of Natasha's last book. Here are a few pages. You know her work better than anyone. Tell me what you think."

Piper heaved a long-suffering sigh, but curiosity must have gotten the better of her. She picked up the pages and began to read. She wasn't even halfway through the first page when her face went first white, then red.

"Why, that—"

"Bitch?" I offered helpfully.

Piper nodded emphatically, her nostrils flaring with hatred.

"So, it is stolen," I said. "I'm guessing you're the one who wrote it."

She turned toward me, eyes wide. "How'd you guess?"

"Your reaction. I mean it was clear Natasha didn't write this. I've read her work. No way she came up with this. It's too beautiful. Too emotional."

Piper perked up, looking almost chipper for the first time since I met her. "You really think so?"

"I know so. Why didn't you try to get it published? Or publish it yourself? It's clear you have the talent."

The anger was back. She shoved the papers at me. "Natasha. I thought she'd give me good feedback, you know. She is, was, a best seller, after all. And it was before me and Jason."

I nodded in encouragement, carefully sipping from my own mug.

"Instead, she told me it was a piece of garbage, and I should give up the ludicrous dream of writing."

Piper's jaw tightened. "I might have known she'd steal my work. This is pretty much word for word."

"You didn't know about it, then?" I found it hard to believe, but then again Piper wasn't Natasha's PA anymore. Plus Natasha could be sneaky.

"Of course not, or I'd have sued the—"

"Bitch," I finished.

She sighed. "Natasha would have probably gotten away with it. I don't read her drivel anymore since it's not my job. She knows it, too. Knew it. She could have published this, and I would have never found out. But why? She makes millions. Why would she steal my book?"

"Because it's good. No, scratch that, it's amazing." I had a feeling Piper was telling the truth. She really didn't know Natasha had stolen her work.

She flushed. "Thanks. But I guess good only gets so far." She sighed again.

"Natasha's publisher was going to publish this under Natasha's name," I said. "They clearly want the book."

"Yeah. Because they think Natasha wrote it. Natasha's name would sell a takeout menu."

I pondered that. "True. But they have to know how good it is. I know some people. Let me talk to them. Perhaps something can be worked out. Or, if you prefer, you could always self-publish. That's how I make my living."

"You'd do that for me?" She seemed a bit suspicious. Couldn't say I blamed her.

"Of course," I assured her. "I'm not one of those writers who believes other writers are my competition. There's plenty enough to go around, believe me."

"Thanks," she said with a small smile, sipping her massive mug of coffee.

I nodded and returned to my own coffee. I didn't let her see my disappointment. Because if Piper hadn't killed Natasha for stealing her story—which she didn't because she didn't even know it had happened—then I was back to square one.

Chapter 19
Something Wicked this Way Slithers

The talk on trends in historical romance—yes, I know how ironic that sounds—was as interesting and informative as I hoped it would be. I even got to meet some of my fellow historical romance writers, whom I'd only talked to online or whose books I'd read and admired. I was feeling particularly star struck as I met Maisie Williams, basically historical's version of Natasha Winters. Except Maisie was gracious, humble, and totally hilarious with her broad New Jersey accent and layers of silk shawls and jet beads. I wasn't sure if her hair was real or a wig, but it was big and blond and tightly curled in a way that hadn't been "in" since the eighties. She wore another silk scarf tied artfully in a band around her forehead. She looked like an old carnival fortune teller. I half expected her to whip out a tarot deck and offer to read my fortune.

I told her I'd enjoyed her latest book and how big a fan I was. She squealed in excitement and, in a loud, nasal voice to rival Maggie's, said, "Sweetheart, I love it. You made my day." Only "sweetheart" came out more like "sweethaht" and "day" had at least one extra syllable.

Maisie patted me on the back and launched into a story about the time she met her own author heroine, Dame Barbara Cartland. "You wouldn't believe it," she said, slapping me on the shoulder, "but she was a lovely woman. Lovely. No airs or graces *at all*. So genuine and down to earth, you couldn't help but just love her. Of course, she had her opinions, let me tell you, and she wasn't exactly the pillar of feminism, but really, *such* a character."

I finally extracted myself from Maisie and headed back to my room for a nap. I had two hours before the next class I wanted to attend, so I'd decided to catch up on some much-needed sleep. All this investigating really took it out of a person.

Tossing my dress over a convenient chair, I threw on my pajamas and climbed into bed, snuggling into the plump pillows with a sigh. The Egyptian cotton sheets were smooth and cool against my overheated skin, and I was soon headed toward dreamland. I was just drifting off when something brushed against my foot. Something muscular and scaly. I froze. It moved again. A glance at the shape beneath the duvet and I knew exactly what it was. Snake.

Spiders were my personal kryptonite. Snakes weren't far off, but I'd seen enough documentaries to know that shrieking and carrying on are surefire ways of getting bitten. Keeping absolutely still could save my life.

My phone lay on the bedside table, so I reached out carefully, one slow inch at a time, and grabbed it. I dialed the first number that came up.

"Hey, Viola. What's up?"

"Cheryl, I need you to be calm."

"Why are you whispering?"

"Someone put a snake in my bed."

Shéa MacLeod

There was a shriek from the other end of the line that nearly deafened me. I winced. "I told you to keep calm."

"I hate snakes." There was an edge of panic in her voice.

"I realize this," I whispered, "but you're not the one in bed with one."

There was a pause. "Good point. Blame the lack of coffee. What should I do?"

"There are poisonous snakes in Florida, and I can't see it. It's under the duvet, so I can't move. Go to the front desk, get the manager. Tell him what's happening. If he doesn't take you seriously, get Lucas to help." People had a way of listening to Lucas Salvatore. "There should be somebody that knows what to do." At least I sure hoped so.

It felt like hours, but was probably only about fifteen minutes, before I heard someone outside my door. The snake had curled right up against my leg, apparently enjoying my body heat. Oh goodie.

There was a light knock. The door handle rattled slightly, and the door swung open. A strange man with bushy brown hair poked his head in. "Ms. Roberts?" he said softly. He was wearing a khaki uniform and an official-looking badge. I didn't bother answering. "My name is Brian. I'm with Fish and Wildlife. I'm going to help you. I just need you to keep absolutely still, okay?"

I shot him a glare. What did he think I'd been doing? Keeping still was not nearly as easy as it sounded. It was downright painful, actually. Plus I had to pee.

178

Brian moved cautiously toward the bed, clearly assessing the situation. "Okay, Ms. Roberts, this is going to be difficult as I can't see the snake to tell if it's venomous, and it's obviously right up against you. So, what I'm going to do is real quick-like stick this sheet of metal," he held up what looked like a cookie sheet, "between you and the snake. That way if it strikes, it won't hit you, right?"

I nodded very slightly. It seemed risky, but what else could I do? Not a lot of options as far as I could see.

"Minute that happens you roll out of bed and onto the floor quick as you can. Then I can contain the snake. Ready?"

Another slight nod. *As I'll ever be.*

Without further ado, Brian slammed the thin sheet of metal right down between my leg and the snake until it hit the mattress. I didn't wait. I rolled so fast I hit the floor hard enough to leave bruises. Brian dropped the metal sheet and whipped up the duvet, catching the snake in it like a sack, before hauling it unceremoniously from the room. I followed him in time to watch as he dumped it into a bucket and slammed down the lid.

"Oh my word, that's a coral snake," I gasped. I knew that coral snakes were super venomous. I would have died if it had bit me.

Brian grinned. "Naw, ma'am. It's just a little ole king snake. Get mistaken for corals all the time, but they're totally harmless." He lifted the container. "I'll take this little honey out to the wild and set him free. Don't you worry."

Frankly, I was less worried about the snake than about me. "How'd it get in my bed? Surely they're not just wandering around hotel rooms at random."

"No, ma'am," he said grimly. "Somebody had to have put him there. You're lucky, if they'd have gotten a real coral snake—"

"I know," I interrupted him. It would have been ugly, to say the least.

"Of course, maybe whomever it was knew the snake was harmless and just wanted to scare you. Either way, looks like you got yourself an enemy." He looked very grim as he said it.

Seriously. He had no idea.

The minute he was gone, a whole entourage tumbled into my room. First came Cheryl followed by Lucas, Maggie, Lu, and finally a strange man I'd never seen before. Cheryl was babbling incoherently and crying, not that I blamed her. I felt like crying myself. Lucas was stony eyed. The strange man was wringing his hands and muttering sympathetic nonsense. Maggie was barking out orders, which no one was listening to, while Lu quietly poured a very large glass of whisky from a flask she'd dug out of her floral beach back and shoved it in my hand. I downed it in two gulps, feeling immediately better.

"Everyone, shut up!" I shouted over the melee. Everyone shut up. I turned to the stranger. He was wearing a rumpled white shirt with a ghastly green and yellow tie. His reddish-brown hair was sprinkled with gray, thinning on top, and his freckled face had seen an unfortunate amount of sun. "You first. Who are you?"

"George O'Malley. Manager. I can't apologize enough, Ms. Roberts. This has never happened before. Not in the history of the resort. Shocking. Truly shocking. Do you need a doctor?"

"No. As you can see I'm in one piece. I could use more booze though." I gave a mournful look at my empty glass.

"I shall take care of it immediately. And the rest of your stay will be comped." He gave me an eager look.

"Okay. Thanks." It wasn't his fault. Obviously someone was out to get me, but hey... free stuff is always good.

With more assurances this wouldn't happen again and overly flowery apologies, George finally left. Thank goodness. I turned to my friends.

"I'm fine, everyone. Really. Just a bit of a surprise."

"I'll say," Maggie said dryly. "Kind of surprise a body could do without."

"I think maybe someone is trying to kill you," Cheryl said soberly.

"Well, they didn't do a very good job since they used the wrong snake," Maggie pointed out.

"Unless they used the right snake," Lucas reminded her, "and were going for the scare not the kill. It could have been a warning."

Maggie snorted. "After the first attempt on her life? I don't think so."

I sighed. "Either way, we really need to find out what is going on. I'm betting whoever left the snake is the same person who pushed me down the stairs. And whoever that is had something to do with both Natasha's and Andrea's deaths." I sank down on the couch, my glass magically refilled. I tossed it back, feeling the pleasant numbness steal over me. It was better than the sheer panic I had been feeling. "What I really need to find out is: who was Andrea's boyfriend?"

"Oh, that's easy," Cheryl said with a grin. "It was that bartender. Kyle."

Chapter 20
Confronting Evil

"What?" I shrieked. "How long have you known this?"

"Since last night," she said calmly. "Max told me. He saw them together when he first arrived at the resort. They were kissing. And then again right before Andrea's death. That time they were arguing. Andrea slapped him across the face."

"When were you going to tell me?" I demanded.

"This morning. Except the whole snake thing sort of got in the way."

She had a point. I drew in a deep breath. "Okay. Okay. Let me think this over..." Things were definitely clicking now. Little pieces that hadn't made sense until now were finally falling into place.

"Interesting development," Lucas murmured. Maggie and Lu nodded in agreement.

"It still doesn't make sense," Cheryl said.

I blinked. "What doesn't?"

"What does Kyle being Andrea's boyfriend have to do with Natasha getting killed? Maybe the two murders aren't related after all."

Maggie snorted.

"Oh, they are," I said. "They most definitely are." I grabbed my maxi dress from the chair and yanked it on over my head, pajamas and all. I snatched my key card from the dresser, thought momentarily about grabbing my handbag, too, but dismissed it.

"Where are you going?" Cheryl demanded as I marched toward the door.

"I need to talk to Kyle. Now."

"But..." she sputtered, "you're not even properly dressed."

"No time." I shoved open the door and marched down the walkway, Cheryl hot on my heels. Lucas wasn't far behind with Lu and Maggie trotting along eagerly.

"Listen. Viola. I know you're on a mission to prove your innocence—" Cheryl started.

"*Our* innocence."

"Right. Sure. But don't you think you should call Detective Costa?"

I snorted. "He'd just screw it up. The man clearly doesn't know his head from his tailpipe."

"But Viola—."

I whirled to face her. "Listen to me, Cheryl. I've got to do this, okay? I've got to know the truth." I didn't bother waiting for her reply. I marched on, determined. It was time to finish this.

# # #

"Where's Kyle?" I barked imperiously at the bartender, a young woman with a dark pixie cut and a cute pair of silver-rimmed glasses. I hadn't seen her before.

She blinked. "Er...who's asking?"

"A friend." Might be a stretch—okay, more than a stretch—but what did she know? I tapped my foot impatiently and gave her my best authoritarian stare.

She pointed at a door marked employees only. "But you can't go in there."

"Watch me." I marched over and threw open the door. It led into a short hallway. Very depressing with utilitarian off-white tiles and matching walls. The overhead fluorescents flickered ominously. Or maybe that was just me. I had been accused once or twice of having an overactive imagination.

To the right were two doors clearly marked as restrooms. Straight ahead, a fire door led to what was likely the outside. On the left was an open doorway leading into a small kitchen/breakroom area. Kyle was sitting alone at one of the tables, eating breakfast.

"Kyle." I stopped in front of him. "We need to talk."

He gave me a once-over, his expression startled. "Are you all right, miss?"

I glanced down at myself realizing for the first time what I sight I must make in my white and blue striped pajamas underneath my brown and turquoise maxi dress. "Yes. Busy morning is all. Can we talk?"

He glanced around. There were half a dozen other people in the room watching us with interest. This suited me fine, but he clearly didn't want an audience.

"Let's go outside," he suggested.

"Fine. Whatever." I followed him into the hall and through the fire door. Outside was a small covered patio with a picnic bench and a collection of cheap plastic ashtrays. Clearly the designated smoking spot. A narrow wooden gate opened to the lush resort grounds. Kyle led me through the gate and down one of the more overgrown paths. Frankly, the Fairwinds needed to rethink their groundskeepers. The path opened up into what must be the overflow storage for beach toys. Kayaks, paddle boats, and other items littered the ground around a small shed that looked stuffed to the gills. Most of the items appeared worn and in need of repair.

"Now, what did you want to talk about?" Kyle stood, legs braced apart, arms crossed over his chest. He looked like a sullen teenager.

"I just found out some interesting information."

He quirked an eyebrow, looking only mildly interested. "Yeah? What?"

I gave him a cool look. "Seems you and Andrea Schwartz, the second murder victim, were an item."

He rolled his eyes. "That's old news. We broke up ages ago."

"Really? Because I have a witness that saw you kissing her just a few days ago. Right before you took up with Natasha, in fact."

He shrugged. "We hooked up. So what?"

"So, the same witness saw you arguing with Andrea just a short while before her murder."

A muscle flexed in his jaw, and his lips grew tight. "Lots of people fight. It's no big deal."

"Really? You break up with one woman to date another only to have the second one get murdered. Then

186

you argue with the first, and she's murdered. It's curious, don't you think?"

He shrugged again, trying to appear nonchalant, but his eyes were dark and angry. I was definitely hitting a nerve.

"Not to mention this." I pulled the small silver bracelet out of my pocket. "Interesting that you pretended not to know who it belonged to."

His eyes narrowed. "What of it. It's none of your business anyway, you old busybody."

I resisted the urge to smack the brat. "I'm certain it's something Detective Costa would be interested in hearing about. Where I found it. *When* I found it"

"So tell him. What do I care? You can't prove anything. Why would I kill Natasha anyway? She was my ticket out of this dump."

Bingo!

"Because you didn't mean to kill Natasha."

He turned sheet white. "I don't know what you're talking about." But some of the belligerence was gone. In its place was a panicked kid who was in way over his head.

"Oh, I think you do," I said, going in for the kill. "You see, that's what stumped me. Why you would kill Natasha. Andrea, I get, but Natasha? Didn't make sense. At least, not until I figured it out."

"Figured what out?" Some of the cockiness was back.

"That you never meant to kill Natasha. Natasha was a mistake. You were supposed to meet Andrea, but she was late, and Natasha showed up first. In the dark, away from the lights of the resort, you couldn't tell the difference. Same color hair. Same height and build. The only difference was their ages, and with Natasha's back turned..." I shrugged. "Woopsie."

"You don't know what you're talking about," he hissed. His face was a contorted mask of anger.

"Don't I? Because I'm guessing that Andrea did eventually show up, and she saw what you did." I held up the bracelet again so that it sparkled in the sunlight. "Andrea saw you kill Natasha, but she didn't get it. She didn't realize you meant to kill *her*. What did she do, Kyle? Blackmail you? Is that how you found out?"

He growled. "No, you idiot. She never said a word. I found out when you came around waving that thing in my face." He pointed at the bracelet. "That's when I knew she'd seen me. It's your fault she's dead."

I felt suddenly sick to my stomach. Rather than go to the cops, I'd tried to solve things myself, and it had gotten Andrea killed. I shook my head. I couldn't think that way. "No, it isn't, Kyle. The only fault here is yours. I'm guessing that was what the argument was about. You had to kill her so she couldn't tell anyone what she'd seen. What I don't quite understand is why you tried to kill Andrea in the first place."

"Don't you, Miss Know-It-All?" Kyle snarled. In his hand was a wicked-looking knife. It looked just like the one I found in Natasha's back. I froze, suddenly realizing just how alone we were. "Andrea was in my way. She threatened to tell Natasha the truth."

"That, uh, you were using her for her money?" I ventured.

"Whatever. Like she wasn't using me." He moved closer, the light glinting of the sharp edge of his blade. "I needed her. Natasha. She was going to get me out of this hellhole."

"I get it. I do. But murder? Seems extreme."

"I couldn't risk it. I needed Natasha. And her money. And then the stupid woman has to go and get herself killed." His face twisted until it was an ugly parody of itself.

Keep him talking. Keep him talking. Somebody has to come by at some point.

"But why did you push me down the stairs? It was you, wasn't it?"

He twirled the knife in his hand, the blade flashing hypnotically. "You were getting a little too close. I thought you might know what the bracelet meant. I couldn't risk you finding out the truth. How could I know you were so slow?"

Ouch. That hurt.

"What can I say? I'm new at this," I said, trying to act nonchalant. "But the snake? Why a king snake?"

He growled. "Idiot sold it to me said it was a coral. Just goes to show you gotta do things yourself. Can't trust anybody. And I definitely can't trust you and your big mouth." He advanced on me, that sharp knife pointed at me like it, and he, meant business.

"Um, Kyle, think about this..."

"I am thinking about it and if you're gone, no one will figure it out."

"What?" I laughed weakly. "You think I'm the only one who figured it out?"

"Yes, Miss Nosey, I do."

"Detective Costa—"

"Is an idiot," he snapped. "Couldn't find his backside with both hands."

Well, I wouldn't have gone that far. Even if I was still irked at him for considering me a suspect.

Kyle lunged at me, and I stepped backward, tripping over a loose bit of debris. I toppled to the sand, scrabbling to get away, to find a weapon. Anything to fend him off. My hand closed around something solid. As Kyle lunged again, I whipped up the kayak paddle and bashed him in the head just as a horde of policemen burst from the bushes, shouting to freeze in the name of the law.

Kyle toppled to the ground, unconscious. I dropped the paddle and held up my hands. Detective Costa loomed over me, glaring.

Chapter 21
Farewell to Fairwinds

It was the last day of the conference, and Lucas had taken Cheryl, Maggie, Lu, and me out for drinks at the Flying Fish. Cheryl had invited Max, but he had to catch an early plane to Boston. Cheryl was looking a little down, so I made a mental note to cheer her up later.

We all gathered around one of the Flying Fish's long tables with humongous wine glasses filled to the brim. There was both a feeling of excitement and sadness. Excitement that the murder was solved and sadness that tomorrow we'd be going our separate ways.

"To Viola," Lucas said, lifting his glass. The look he gave me was rife with meaning.

"Viola!" the others chimed in.

"All right, girl, spill," Maggie demanded. "When did you know it was Natasha's boy toy?"

"When Cheryl told me that Kyle was Andrea's boyfriend. I mean, it made sense, him killing her. Get her out of the way and all. But not him killing Natasha. Unless it was an accident. Then I recalled once seeing Andrea in the lobby. I thought at first it was Natasha, they're so similar, at least from behind. I realized that if I could mistake them, the killer might have, too, especially in the dark. And if that were the case, it explained both murders."

"Smart thinking," Lucas said approvingly.

"I still think you're an idiot," Cheryl snapped. "You could have been killed!"

"But I wasn't," I said reassuringly. "I knew I could count on you to call Detective Costa. Unfortunately he ran a bit later than I'd hoped," I said wryly, "but it all worked out in the end."

"Let me get this straight," Lu said. "Kyle wanted to kill Andrea because she was planning to tell Natasha that Kyle was only into the relationship for the money?"

"Exactly," I said. "He was stupid enough to believe Natasha planned on taking him with her when she left Florida."

"As if that would happen," Cheryl said. "Natasha would have ditched him the minute the conference was over."

"You and I know that," I agreed, "but Kyle didn't know her like we did. Of course, once he accidentally killed Natasha, he *had* to kill Andrea," I said.

"Because she witnessed it, of course," Lucas surmised.

I nodded. "And if her fate wasn't sealed before, it was then. When he saw the bracelet, he decided Andrea had to die. He couldn't risk her telling anyone what she'd seen."

"That's just nuts," Maggie snapped. "What is the world coming to?"

"What about the plagiarized book?" Lucas asked. "The one Natasha was trying to pass off as her own."

That involved another round of explanation. "The publishing company has now seen proof that Piper is the author. Greta has backed her up. Even Yvonne finally admitted her part in the theft. So the publishing company fired Yvonne, voided Natasha's contract for the plagiarized book, and issued one to Piper. They're going to publish the book, but the right way."

"That's wonderful!" Lu gushed, clasping her hands over her ample bosom. "I'm so pleased."

"Hopefully Piper doesn't turn into another Natasha," Maggie muttered over her glass of wine. She didn't sound hopeful. I wondered if Piper would stick with Jason once she was a successful author. I kind of doubted it, but then people had a way of surprising you.

The night finally wound to a close, and we all bid each other goodnight, promising to stay in touch. As the others headed to bed, Lucas pulled me aside.

"I'd love to see you again," he said softly, looking at me as if he wanted to kiss me on the lips again. This time on purpose.

"I don't see how that's possible," I said. "We live so far away."

"Portland isn't that far from Astoria. It's what? An hour-and-a-half drive or so? Two max."

I blinked. "Wait. What? Portland? As in Oregon? I thought you lived in New Hampshire or something."

"Maine. But I've decided it's time for a change." He flashed me one of those sexy grins. "How about it, Viola? Dinner when we get back?"

# # #

The next morning, Cheryl and I checked out of the Fairwinds Resort and headed to the front entrance, luggage in hand, to catch a taxi. Instead, an unmarked police car slid to the curb, and Costa got out. He was looking particularly delicious in a rumpled, sky-blue shirt, his maroon tie askew.

"Why, Detective," I called cheerfully, giving him a little finger wave. "Come to see us off? I know you're going to miss me, but really, you needn't have."

He glared at me as if I were personally responsible for all his woes. "Actually, I'm giving you a ride to the airport."

"Really?" I bit back a laugh. "Why would you do that?"

"Because my captain ordered me to," he said, his tone nearly a growl. "He said, 'Get that Roberts person off my island before I have her thrown in jail.' I wouldn't have cared, except he also threatened my person."

"Well," I said with a grin as I strolled toward his car, "you can't say my visit wasn't interesting."

Cheryl and I ignored Costa's glare as we burst into peals of laughter. Hey, at least we'd save on cab fare.

The End

Join Viola on her next adventure in *The Stiff in the Study,* available May 2016.

A Note From Shéa MacLeod

Thank you for reading The Corpse in the Cabana. If you enjoyed this book, I'd appreciate it if you'd help others find it so they can enjoy it too.

Please return to the site where you purchased this book and leave a review to let other potential readers know what you liked or didn't like about The Corpse in the Cabana.

Book updates can be found at www.sheamacleod.com

Be sure to sign up for my mailing list so you don't miss out!
http://sheamacleod.com/mailing-list-2/

You can follow Shéa MacLeod on Facebook
https://www.facebook.com/shea.macleod or on Twitter under @Shea_MacLeod.

Shéa MacLeod

About Shéa MacLeod

Shéa MacLeod is the author of urban fantasy, post-apocalyptic, scifi, paranormal romances with a twist of steampunk. She also dabbles in contemporary romances with a splash of humor. She resides in the leafy green hills outside Portland, Oregon where she indulges in her fondness for strong coffee, Ancient Aliens reruns, lemon curd, and dragons.

Because everything's better with dragons.

Other Books by Shea Shéa MacLeod

Notting Hill Diaries
To Kiss a Prince
Kissing Frogs
Kiss Me, Chloe
Kiss Me, Stupid
Kissing Mr. Darcy
Cupcake Goddess Novelettes
Be Careful What You Wish For
Nothing Tastes As Good
Soulfully Sweet
A Stich in Time
Sunwalker Saga
Kissed by Blood- February 2016
Kissed by Darkness
Kissed by Fire
Kissed by Smoke
Kissed by Moonlight
Kissed by Ice
Kissed by Eternity
Sunwalker Saga: Soulshifter Trilogy
Fearless
Haunted
Soulshifter
Sunwalker Saga: Witch Blood Series
Spellwalker
Deathwalker
Mistwalker (coming Summer 2016)
Dragon Wars
Dragon Warrior
Dragon Lord
Dragon Goddess
Green Witch
Omicron ZX
Omicron Zed-X: Omicron ZX prequel Novellette
A Rage of Angels

Printed in Great Britain
by Amazon